KANSAS KISSED

ROMANCE ACROSS STATE LINES

DEBBIE WHITE

ISBN 9781729164372 – KDP PAPERBACK

ISBN 978-1-7363803-7-6– INGRAM SPARK PAPERBACK

KANSAS KISSED

Editing by Daniela Prima from Prima Editing & Proofreading Services

&

Leo Bricker The Grammatical Eye®

Cover Design by Larry White

Another school year was ending, and the only thing that was going to make this summer even a little bit brighter was the trip she'd won. It weighed heavily on her mind, only because she'd never been so bold to travel anywhere by herself. This was a first, but the timing felt right. So much had happened in a few short years. Good things for the most part. There was always some baggage you must carry, though, right? You have to trudge through the icky stuff life tosses at you to get to the light at the end of the tunnel. Dodge City just might be that light.

Lucy looked up when she heard some commotion and found her friend and colleague, Beth, struggling with a large clear container. "I'm ready, are you?"

"Just about." Lucy pushed back her chair, the one

she'd occupied for the entire school year, and stood. "It's always strange for me," she said, lowering her head.

"I know. Part of me is like, *yes*, summer is here, bring on the margaritas, and then the other part of me is like, I'm sure going to miss all the smiling faces eager to learn." Beth sighed as she shifted the container in her arms.

Lucy tossed a few more things into her own plastic container and carried her load to the door. She gave one last look around the empty classroom before turning off the lights and then stepped back, allowing the spring-loaded door to close, concluding another satisfying year at Denver Elementary.

The hall echoed with their voices as they exited the school. There were no little voices yelling in joyful banter to drown them out. The only sounds besides their soft voices were their heels as they clicked down the well-worn grey linoleum, which was marked with black scuffs from the children's shoes as they roughhoused daily before the bell rang. Something the janitorial crew would rectify at some point over the summer with their indus-trial-size buffers. Those scuffed tiles would shine after they were through, and would welcome all the returning students and faculty, as well as any new faces, come the fall.

"Well, here we are," Lucy said, hitting the key fob to

release her trunk. She gingerly set the overflowing container in her sparse trunk and stepped back.

Struggling to find room in her packed trunk, Beth finally found a space to slide her container into. "I never know if I should be happy or sad about this day. When do you leave for your trip?"

"Two weeks from tomorrow," Lucy answered as she wiped a speck of dirt off of her newly washed car.

"I can't wait to hear all about it." Beth slammed the door to her trunk, and then moved around the corner, resting her back against her car. "One of these days, I'm going to get a new car with one of those fancy door openers." She grinned widely at her pal.

The shiny white Prius had been a gift from Lucy's parents. She'd never asked for, nor had she expected it, but they'd said they would rather see her reap some of the benefits of their hard-earned money while they were still around.

"I'm a little nervous about the whole Dodge City trip," Lucy said, shielding her eyes from the intense afternoon sun.

"Why? It's an all-expense paid trip. What's there to be concerned about?"

"It's so not me, though, you know?" Lucy shrugged.

"I know, but it's what you need to do, Lucy. We've talked about that. Cut loose, do something out of the ordinary for a change." Beth flashed a wide smile at her friend, giving Lucy a glimpse of her newly acquired braces.

"By the way, how are you adjusting to the braces?"

"I'm doing alright. They are a pain taking them out every time I want to eat, but I think overall these are way better than the metal kind. Have you finished packing yet?"

"I've tried to finish packing, but you know me. Everything must coordinate." She looked down at her blue and white checkered button-down blouse, dark jeans, and blue Keds.

Beth tossed her head back and laughed. "You'll be fine. Just toss those clothes in there and go have a blast. I'll be thinking about you enjoying the rodeo while I visit my parents in boring Idaho." She walked over to Lucy and held out her arms.

They promised to get together and share their stories, even though Beth was convinced Lucy would have the most exciting ones to share. A small part of Lucy wished she was going to boring Idaho with her friend instead of to Dodge City.

Lucy got into her car and started the engine. She watched her friend back out, and then began the twenty-minute drive to her apartment, making a mental list of what she still had to accomplish. Besides packing, there was alerting the post office to hold her mail, give all her houseplants a good watering, and let's see … oh, yes, have lunch with her parents. How could she forget that?

"HELLO? MOM? DAD?" Lucy called out as she let herself in.

"We're out here," her mom replied.

Lucy carefully placed her purse on the couch, taking care not to mess up her mom's tidy pillow arrangement or spill any contents from her purse, and moved toward the back of the house where the kitchen and dining area were located. Through the French doors that led to the covered patio, she could see her parents busily setting the outdoor table. She opened the door and stepped outside.

"Lucy, dear, how are you?" Her mother gave her a peck on the cheek as she folded napkins.

"Good." Her eyes wandered to the explosion of color in the backyard her mother painstakingly took care of. "Your roses are beautiful," she commented.

"I got pricked by one of those rascals," her dad said with a twinkle in his eyes as he held up his thumb as proof.

Lucy's mom pursed her lips. "And we'll be hearing about that injury for a long time, right, Paul?" She laughed as she continued to move around the glass and wrought iron table.

"Marjorie, it hurt like the dickens."

Lucy followed behind her mother, straightening plates and silverware. She loved order as much as her mother did. "Who else is coming?" She quickly noted the extra place setting.

Her mother lifted her head, their eyes meeting. "I invited Josh. I hope you don't mind."

Lucy arched her brows. "Mom, we've been over this before."

"He's such a nice fellow. It's just lunch."

Paul came around the table and swung his big arm over Lucy's shoulders, pulling her in for a hug. He gave her a peck on the cheek, and then smiling, winked at her. "It's just lunch," he whispered before freeing her.

She breathed in slowly and counted to ten as she exhaled. "It's just lunch," she repeated, nodding her head.

It worked out fine. Josh came, they talked about their summer plans, and when he hinted about maybe going out on a date or something, and she ignored him, he politely excused himself from her presence and talked to her dad for the rest of the afternoon. It suited her just fine. She had absolutely no interest in him, whatsoever. He talked about business strategy until she became cross-eyed. Talk about predictable and boring; Josh took the cake. It was no wonder her mom thought they'd make a good match, but there was such a thing as opposites attracting for a reason. Even Lucy could see that.

"Help me in the kitchen, Lucy," her mother requested.

Marjorie sliced the pound cake while Lucy retrieved the sliced strawberries and whipped cream.

"I won't ever invite him again. I promise." Marjorie carefully removed cake slices with a spatula as she peered out into the yard through the window over the sink.

"Okay," Lucy said, scooping strawberries out of the bowl and gently spreading them across each slice of pound cake.

"I just wish you'd find a fellow and settle down. Dad and I—"

"Mom," Lucy said, not letting her mother finish. "We've been through this before. I'm not looking to settle down. I love teaching, and coming home—"

"To a lonely apartment?" her mother interrupted her this time.

"Anyway," Lucy said, determined to change the subject. "I'm sort of excited about this Kansas trip."

"I wish someone was going with you."

"The contest prize was for just one, but it's such a nice package—hotel, food vouchers, tickets to the rodeo, and more." She dolloped whipped cream on each dessert.

"Well, I'm glad you're excited, but let me just say,

Kansas isn't all that. It's dusty, flat, and out in the middle of nowhere." Her mother washed her hands under the faucet.

Lucy twisted her mouth in a tight knot. She didn't want to contradict her mother, but all the pictures she'd seen showed her something quite different. She also didn't want to admit she was extremely hesitant about going. That would only make matters worse. Her mother would become frantic with worry knowing Lucy was anxious, and then before you know it, they'd both be spun up so much it would take a gallon of calming tea, or Paul, to lower the boom on them to get them to listen to reason.

They each carried two plates of the eye-catching dessert outside.

"This sure is delicious," Josh said, eagerly digging in.

Lucy smiled. Then she noticed the little dab of whipped cream that sort of just clung to the corner of his mouth. She wanted to reach up and wipe it away with her napkin. She kept staring at it, wondering why he didn't feel that substance just sitting there. She finally looked away. It bothered her that much.

She hated her compulsive behavior. It was the one thing she wished she could change about herself. So many little things just bugged the heck out of her. She tried taking deep breaths, thinking about other things, but nope, whatever it was that irritated her, came right back, front and center.

Josh left after dessert, but not before expressing his gratitude for his invitation. He casually nodded to Lucy and wished her well with her summer plans and then took off.

LUCY CHUCKLED at the sight of both of her parents' smiling faces squeezed into the opening of the passenger window.

"Now, you be careful around all those cowboys, Lucy Carmichael," her dad playfully warned.

Marjorie laughed. "Take lots of pictures. Call us and let us know you made it safely. That's a long drive for a single lady to make all by herself."

"Mom, it's only a six-hour drive!"

"I know, but it's still a long drive by yourself," Marjorie said in her most motherly voice.

"I'm a little nervous, I'll admit it. This is a big thing for me, but I need you to feel confident that I can do this." A tear formed on her bottom lid.

Paul reached in through the window and stroked his daughter's hand. "You can do it. I have faith in you." He winked at her, making her smile.

Her parents backed out of the window and stood on the sidewalk, waving at her as she drove away. She brushed away that stubborn tear that managed to trail down her cheek, and headed to her apartment, all the while mumbling, "Yes, I can. Yes, I can."

CHAPTER 2

She stood in front of her closet for at least five minutes, debating which blouses she wanted to pack for her trip. "Why does this have to be so difficult for me?" She grabbed a white blouse off the hanger and tossed it onto the bed.

She went through her closet, flipping through tops, and then after what was even too long for her, began pulling random blouses off hangers and tossing them onto the bed, right along with the white one.

As far back as she could remember, she'd always paid great attention to detail. Maybe a bit excessively, but she couldn't help it. Even while attending summer camp with the Scouts, they had teased her because she had the best rolled sleeping bag, and her clothes always looked like they'd just come from the cleaners. It was all in the way you folded them she'd told them.

She made sure the heavy items like pants were on the bottom— key to keeping things neatly arranged. Then she meticulously folded her tops, making sure no wrinkles would come from a sloppy fold, before gently laying them in her suitcase. Next, she rolled up her tee shirts and stacked them inside a large ziplock plastic bag. A trick she'd learned from the internet. Blowing a strand of hair out of her face, she did the same with her underwear.

After she finished packing, she made herself a cup of chamomile tea and settled in to watch some of the television shows she'd recorded. She'd hit the road early to beat the Denver morning traffic, and should arrive in Dodge City by lunchtime if everything worked out the way she planned.

WITH THE RUGGED terrain as her viewing pleasure, Lucy made her way through the various elevations as she traveled toward Kansas. The wildflowers were colorful additions to the purple mountains, and the calm blue sky offered serenity to her already overworking mind. She tried to enjoy the scenery, but Dodge City and what awaited her conjured a bunch of new what-ifs, and soon her anxiety blurred the vision of the beautiful scenery.

She'd packed bottled water along with some snacks, and when her tummy told her it was time for a break, she pulled over at a rest stop to stretch her legs and use the bathroom. To her surprise, she had phone service, and checked the weather app on her phone to see if the forecast had changed in Dodge City. She'd checked that morning, but that was part of her OCD, checking and rechecking things.

When she saw a text from her mother, she laughed. "Are you there yet?"

"No, Mom, I'm not there yet," she texted back.

The rest of the trip was pretty mundane. After leaving Colorado, the geography began to change. It went from pretty mountainous to gently rolling hills with areas of flatness in between. She rather liked this change to the layout of the land.

She followed the directions on her electronic mapping system in her car and it took her right to the front door of the hotel. She'd already scoped out the hotel on their website, so there were no surprises. She parked her car and went inside to register.

"Welcome to Dodge City," the perky clerk said.

"Thank you … Wanda," Lucy replied, noting her name tag.

"Do you have reservations?"

"Yes. My name is Lucy Carmichael."

The clerk studied her computer monitor. "Yes, you're the winner of the contest that the city's tourism department ran." Her eyes lifted to meet Lucy's.

Lucy flashed a warm smile. "Yes. I'm very excited. I've never won anything before."

The clerk typed in a few more things on her keyboard and then produced a paper from the printer, setting it on the counter before handing Lucy a pen. "You'll love it here. There's so much activity going on during our annual celebration. We're so happy to have you here."

Lucy nodded then penned in her car plate information as requested and handed the pen back to Wanda.

"Breakfast is from six o'clock until ten in the dining room. You can order off the menu or have the buffet." She lifted her chin and motioned behind Lucy to where the dining room was located.

Lucy turned around and saw a hallway. She figured the dining area was that way.

"The pool is open until 10:00 p.m. and we also have a Jacuzzi."

"Well, I'll be pretty busy with all the activities, but I'll keep that in mind." Lucy had packed her swimsuit just in case after she saw pictures of the pool on their website.

"Here's your key. Let us know if you need anything. Oh, and here's your package that was left by the tourism committee." Wanda retrieved the large envelope from underneath the counter and pushed it toward Lucy. "Everything you need to know should be in there, but if you have any questions, just let me know." Her wide smile made Lucy feel right at home.

Lucy found her room and settled in. The first thing she did was wipe everything down with the disinfectant wipes she'd brought. Then she pulled the bedspread back and sprayed Lysol. She got on her knees and looked under the bed, and just for good measure, sprayed some underneath there, too. She'd read those bedbugs could be anywhere. She pulled open the heavy drapes to let some light in, and then began to unpack. She set her clothes inside the dresser drawers but not before lining them with sheets of paper she'd brought along and hung up the rest of her clothes, before neatly lining her toiletry items along the bathroom counter. Finally, she sat in the red leather arm chair and looked over her itinerary. This first day she was on her own, but starting in the morning, fun, fun, fun. She sighed and taking a deep breath, repeated, "I can do this. I can do this."

Before she knew it, it was dinnertime. After a quick search on her phone, she settled on a restaurant that had good ratings, and drove to it.

She ordered a Cobb salad, minus the blue cheese, tomatoes, and cucumbers. And instead of the house dressing, she asked for vinaigrette on the side, and an iced tea to drink, unsweetened. She squeezed some sanitizer on her hands, and while she waited, she studied the customers and the plates of food that passed by her booth. Talk about large portions!

She sat in an oversized booth near a window, feeling like a minnow in a large fish tank. Surely there was a smaller table available. Maybe they thought she was expecting guests. She shrugged then turned her attention to outside, scanning the different cars and people that came into her view—men wearing cowboy hats, women wearing short shorts and thin strapped tank tops, old married couples holding hands, and a couple of motorcyclists looking like they were traveling the globe with all the gear they had. One even was pulling a trailer. Dodge City really wasn't that much different than Denver.

Jarring her out of her people watching activity, the waitress asked if she would like any dessert.

"Oh, gosh, dessert sounds good. What would you recommend?"

"The apple pie with vanilla bean ice cream is our customer pick." She held her pencil ready to write up the order.

"Okay, that does sound delicious."

"Coming right up." She scribbled something down and then hurried away.

SHE OVERATE, causing a mild attack of indigestion. *Why did she do that*? Now she'd have to take some medicine to ease her full and uncomfortable stomach or she'd never get any rest. Finally, with the television on, she fell asleep.

Bam. Bam. Bam. Bam.

She stirred in bed.

"Fire! Fire!" someone called from the door.

She tossed the covers back and jumped out of bed, coughing when she drew in a breath with the strong odor of smoke.

"Please evacuate the rooms," a voice bellowed from a speaker.

She grabbed her purse, but realized she wasn't dressed properly to run outside. She snatched up a sweater she'd left neatly folded over the chair arm and threw it on, at least covering her top half, before heading out the door. The lights from the fire engine blinded her, and she squinted as she hurried to the parking area where police and firemen were directing people. She held her purse tightly up to her chest while trying to keep her sweater closed. All she had on was a camisole top and matching cotton shorts that barely covered her bottom. The night air on her legs made her shiver.

After about fifteen minutes, a fireman gave the sign that it was all clear and they could go back to their rooms. "It's okay, folks. The fire was contained to one unit. It started by someone using an unauthorized hot plate. It's safe for you to go back to your rooms."

"Excuse me, sir?" Lucy walked up to the fireman who'd been talking. "I'm a bit confused."

"It's late. You were probably in a deep sleep when we woke you up. It's okay. You can go back to your room."

She stepped back, gripping her sweater tightly. His piercing blue eyes journeyed to her exposed legs, causing her to twist and turn away from him. "No, I get that, but why didn't I hear the sirens?" She shook her head in confusion.

"We always respond with sirens, but to be fair, we turned them off as soon as we pulled into the parking lot. Maybe you had the radio going?" His eyes twinkled as he spoke and she found herself studying his face.

"No …" Her eyes lit up with sudden understanding. "But I had the television on and fell asleep. I guess when the sirens came on I thought it was sounds from the TV."

"That makes sense, I guess." He started to move on.

"Well, that, and I had such an early start to drive the several hours to get here. I was exhausted."

"That can do it." He turned his back on her and started to move away.

"Thank you. Thank you for all you do." She grimaced at her dumb line and her clumsy attempt to flirt with the handsome fireman. Why did she even bother? That wasn't like her, anyway.

"You're welcome, Miss. Have a good evening."

Uncomfortable for having said what she said, all she wanted to do now was escape the situation. She hurriedly moved through the parking lot back to her room. She could still smell a bit of smoke in the air, but it seemed the fire department was on it and little damage was done. As she settled back into bed, the fireman's blue eyes seemed to dance in and out of her consciousness, making it difficult to sleep. Frustrated with her behavior, she rolled over and began counting sheep.

CHAPTER 3

After a light complimentary breakfast, Lucy set off for what would be the start of the ten-day celebration known as Dodge City Days. Her first stop was to the car show and arts and crafts shows.

She meandered down paths, which were nothing more than beaten down straw, while munching on freshly popped corn. She'd stop and admire the shiny cars and nod toward who she assumed were the owners, making some small talk before moving on to the next one. They ranged from vintage cars and trucks to newer sporty convertibles, and although she wasn't what you'd call a car person, she had a keen eye for detail, and these cars were nothing short of art displayed in wheat colored fields. The owners clearly were proud of them; with soft cloths in hand, they wiped down every speck of dust.

This she could relate to. After she felt she'd given the car show enough time, she strolled over to the arts and crafts show.

The same well-walked straw paths greeted her as she stopped at every vendor and eyed their beautiful handiwork. She saw handmade jewelry, quilts, leather goods, homemade dog biscuits, and more. But what really caught her eye was the stained-glass display. She couldn't help herself and bought a small piece in the shape of a cowboy silhouette that had a place to insert a suction cup hanger. It would look nice on her window above her kitchen sink. Her first souvenir perfectly symbolized her time at Dodge City.

After all of her walking, she worked up quite an appetite and found the food trucks mostly by smell. She got in line, but froze when it was her time to place her order at the window. *Was it the hot dog she wanted or the corn dog?* She quickly scanned the menu displayed on a large whiteboard. *Or maybe the chicken on the stick?* "I'll take the corn dog," she said at the last minute, realizing she was holding up progress when the grumpy man behind her sighed loudly at her indecisiveness.

The man handed her a corn dog and nodded toward the tabletop that was secured to the side of his truck. "Condiments are over there," he said in a husky voice.

She took her corn dog over to an empty picnic table

and sat down. At the same time she took a bite, her eyes met a familiar set of eyes. She chewed quickly, wiping her mouth, and setting the corn dog in the disposable holder.

"Oh, hey, it's the fireman." A smile curled on her mouth, realizing once again that another dumb line had emerged from her lips.

"It's the sleepyhead traveler with the nice-looking legs." He sat down across from her.

A quick hard pulse in her throat delayed her response. Eventually, she managed to squeak out a "Ha ha." His blue eyes held her prisoner. Finally, she was able to break their hold and she looked down.

"So, you mentioned you'd driven all day to get here. Where did you come from?"

Lifting her chin when she heard him speak, she offered a shaky smile. *This guy was pretty inquisitive.* "Denver."

"Denver. I've been there a few times. What brings you to Dodge City?"

More bold questions. I guess you have to be pretty confident to be a fireman. "I won a trip here." She clasped her hands in her lap, locking eyes with him once again. Now, she noticed something else. He had the most handsome rugged face and dimples, too.

"Won a trip? That's cool. Well, enjoy your time here."

He got up from the bench and dug his hands in his pockets, rocking back on his heels.

Her eyes traveled down and then up the length of his body, finally resting back on his face. She now noticed his thick, dark hair, his chiseled jaw, and the five o'clock shadow that would normally drive her crazy trying to figure out why he wouldn't just shave it off, and the dimples when he smiled, making it all so perfect. She smiled. "I will, thanks."

He started to turn and move away from the well-worn picnic table, when he suddenly turned back toward her. "By the way, my name is Samuel, but my friends call me Sam." He held out his hand.

"Lucille Carmichael," she said, shaking his hand.

"Lucille Carmichael." He nodded. "I like that. It has a nice ring to it." He held her hand, making her blush.

"My friends call me Lucy. I didn't get your last name."

"Lyons."

She pulled her hand free. "It's nice to meet you, Sam Lyons."

"Are you enjoying your time here in Dodge City so far?" His eyes melted her heart, making it difficult to think straight.

"Yes, I am," she managed to squeak out. "There are so many historical markers here I look forward to seeing," she added, indicating she was aware of the town's famous history.

"Good deal," he said, tipping his head. "Well, I'd say I hope to see you again, maybe, but that would mean another fire, and I wouldn't want that." The corners of his mouth drew up.

She nodded. "True, I wouldn't want that either." She looked off into the distance then turned back toward him. "But, you just never know. We might cross paths again." There, she said it. She wasn't sure why she said it, but it was too late now to take it back.

"Yep, you never know. Well, I'll let you get back to your lunch. I smell something pretty good coming over from that way." He motioned toward the food trucks.

"I couldn't decide. Everything smelled and looked good."

He lowered his gaze to her corn dog. "Well, you can't go wrong with a corn dog." He chuckled. "Nice seeing you. Take care."

"Nice to see you, too. Take it easy."

After he walked away, she steadied her pounding heart by breathing in and out a few times. She looked at the corn dog with one bite missing. She'd lost her appetite after that unexpected but very pleasant visit with Sam. She picked up the corn dog while casually twisting her body toward the direction Sam walked. Her eyes darted above and around the crowds of people walking in both directions. Just when she thought he was gone, she spotted him. His strong muscular thighs and broad shoulders stood out in the sea of people. She tasted another bite of her lunch as she watched him weave in and out of the crowd, her eyes never wavering from his well-defined backside. Practically drooling over his physique, she squinted as he moved deeper into the crowd, tracking him all the way. To catch the last few seconds of him, Lucy rose to her feet. Then he was gone for good.

Lucy had read every detail of the letter the tourism center had sent her when they notified her she'd won. It was a good thing, too, because bringing a folding chair to watch the parade was one of the best pieces of advice she'd been given.

Looking up at the sky and knowing how the sun would drift and set, she tried to find a favorable spot. The sidewalks were already overflowing with parade seekers. Children licking popsicles, eating ice cream cones, and munching on candied apples lined the walks with their parents nearby. This town screamed family friendly, and she loved seeing all the smiling faces.

Floats decorated with streamers, flowers, and other

adornments passed by, making all the children scream in delight. The one they really loved had a Dalmatian riding at the top with a fireman. A fireman! Could that be? Yes, it was! He locked eyes with her and waved. She raised her hand and folded her fingers in a wave, watching him as he passed them all by until she couldn't see the float any longer. Float after float passed by for about an hour, and then the parade ended and everyone folded up their chairs and blankets and went on to other activities.

Looping her chair's carrying strap over her shoulder, she made her way back to her parked car. Her mouth felt parched from the heat and dust, and she looked around to see if she could find a place to get a cool drink. She spotted a little diner, and after putting her chair in the trunk, she headed to it.

Once inside, she found a small empty table, and ordered an iced tea, which a waitress quickly brought to her.

"Well, well, well. It seems we keep bumping into each other." Sam flipped his white wrought iron chair around and straddled the seat, resting his arms along the back.

She pulled her mouth off her straw and smiled. "Yes, it seems so. Or maybe you're following me," she said with a hint of tease in her voice.

He slapped his chest with an open palm. "Who, me?" He laughed.

Her eyes went up to the ball cap he wore with the bill flipped around the back. She wanted to reach over and fix it but she resisted. It did kind of look sexy sitting like that. Then her eyes settled on his shirt with the fireman logo on it, and she noticed he had a couple of coffee stains. She nodded to his shirt. "Cold water immediately after a spill can take those out." She sat back in her chair.

He looked down at his blue shirt with the yellowish circles. "Oh, that. This morning when we were getting the float ready, I spilled coffee."

"Just for future reference." She leaned forward and sipped some more of her iced tea.

"How'd you like the parade?"

"I loved it, especially seeing the smiles on all the children's faces. They really got a kick out of the dog on your float."

"So, you like kids, huh?" He lifted his cap off his head and ran his hand through his dark wavy hair.

Her heart pinged when a wave of hair dropped over his eye a bit. Wow, this man was something else. She looked back down at her drink.

"Let me guess. You're a teacher."

Her head flew up and they locked eyes. "How'd you

know that?" She began to wonder if he really was following her, or even more, asking about her.

"You said you got a kick out of the kids. I just took a guess. I can't read your mind, if that's what you're thinking." He laughed at her.

She'd never admit it, but for a fleeting moment she wondered if he had some crazy magical skills, or maybe … he was a private detective during his time off. "Don't be ridiculous. Of course, I know you can't read minds, silly." She pursed her lips and laced her hands together on her lap.

"Okay, I'll come clean. I don't want you to have a heart attack or something and then I'll have to go into my rescue mode and do mouth-to-mouth. My sister is the clerk at the hotel you're staying at."

Mouth-to-mouth sounded kind of nice. She shook her head. "I wondered if that's where the information came from. Wanda, right?"

"She asked me to pick up the package you'd won from the tourism center. I was on my way to have lunch with her. I couldn't resist, I admit it. I looked to see who this person was that won such a nice prize package."

"So, was your stalker plan in motion before the fire, or is that where your plan was hatched?" She raised her brows as she tried to put it all together. Here she thought it was just a chance meeting.

He offered up his dimples when he smiled. "Oh, now I'm really crushed. A stalker? It was just a coincidence. I didn't even know you were the same girl in the package." He stood and turned his chair back around.

He towered above her and his presence overwhelmed her some. She scooted her chair a little closer to the window, putting some distance between them and peered up at him. "Man, you're tall."

He chuckled. "Six feet three inches. Next to you, I guess I do look really tall. You're such a petite little thing."

The way he said *petite little thing* made the hair on her arms stand straight up. She quickly brushed her arms, trying to calm her nerves. "I'm five feet four inches. That's not that small, is it?" She smiled when he winked at her.

"Have a great day, Miss Lucy." He took his ball cap off, biding her farewell, and then placed it back on his head—the right way.

She finished her iced tea, but the butterflies in her stomach were in a fluttering mess, and so was she.

OVER THE COURSE of the next few days, Lucy revisited the arts and crafts show, poked her head into some cute little shops, and visited a few antique shops as well. Everyone she came in contact with smiled and greeted her. She loved the small-town feeling and it made her feel right at home. Secretly, she hoped she'd run into the fireman, Sam. If he was indeed a stalker, she just might be persuaded to be his next victim!

She drove out to the Wyatt Earp and Doc Holliday statues, where she snapped a bunch of pictures including some selfies with them. She ventured to Longhorn Park and watched in amazement at the cattle grazing on prairie grass. She took a picture of the plaque honoring the millions of wild Texas longhorns driven to the city during the 1870s and 1880s. Her last visit for the day, and perhaps the most memorable, was the Sitting Bull statue.

Tired and hungry from her sightseeing, Lucy headed to the diner she'd visited her first night in town.

The same waitress served her. "Cobb salad without blue cheese, tomatoes, or cucumbers, and vinaigrette on the side?"

Fumbling the menu, Lucy blushed. "You remembered."

The waitress held her pencil, ready to take her order.

"No, I think I'll have something different this time." She felt like breaking out of the mold tonight. "I'll have the cheeseburger without …" She stopped herself. "No, make that a cheeseburger with everything on it except tomatoes and pickles." No matter how much she wanted to break out of the mold, pickles and tomatoes just wouldn't be happening.

"Coming right up."

She wiped her mouth in between bites of the delicious burger, piled high with onions, lettuce, and some drippy sauce.

"No dessert tonight for me," she said to the waitress as she handed her a dinner voucher.

Completely full and tired, she headed back to the hotel. She had a full day ahead tomorrow with a longhorn cattle drive and a barn dance, and it would test her other vice, lack of confidence and social awkwardness.

She fell into bed, and as she watched some local news, her eyes grew heavy. Turning the volume down on the television, she fluffed her pillow just the way she liked it, and rolled over. The phone rang and her eyes flew open.

She scooted up from under the covers and grabbed the phone. "Hello?"

"Hey. I hope you don't mind me calling your room."

She held the receiver to her ear, trying to make sense out of the voice on the other end. "Sam?"

"Yeah, it's me."

"Oh, what time is it?"

"It's about nine o'clock. Did I wake you?"

"I just dozed off. It's been a busy day. What's up?"

"Okay, we've already established I know a lot about you. So, I'm not going to beat around the bush. I know part of the prize package includes the cattle drive and barn dance. I wanted to know if you'd like to go with me."

Her heart pounded in her chest, causing the thumping to ricochet in her eardrums. "Oh, wow. Let's see … hmm …" She didn't want him to know how much his invitation excited her.

"If you'd rather not, then that's okay, too. But I don't have a date for the dance, and seems like you might not either." His soft tone made her snuggle back deep under the covers.

Trying to keep her voice even-keeled and hoping her heart would take notice, she calmly said, "That would be fine. I can meet you somewhere."

"Why don't I just pick you up?"

She swallowed down the lump in her throat and tried to calm her breathing before she replied. If this wasn't a real date, she didn't know what would constitute one. "I'll be ready. I don't like to be late, so pick me up at four, please."

"Yes, ma'am."

"It's just that I don't like to be late," she repeated,

feeling like this was her dumb line number three, or was it four? She'd lost count.

"I know, you said that already—twice." He laughed.

"Good night, Sam," she said.

She held onto the phone a bit longer before hanging up. She wanted to replay the conversation in her head another time or two before she forgot how it went. Who was she fooling? She'd never be able to forget the conversation or him. And yet, she didn't really know why.

CHAPTER 4

Sam didn't ask for too many days off other than his scheduled days off. He was known more for taking extra shifts. When you're single and not attached that's what you did. Then you sock all the overtime away for a rainy day.

But everyone knew when the Dodge City Days celebrations came around, Sam Lyons would take a few days off. He looked forward to all the festivities, and even participated in the parade on his own time.

It'd been a while since he'd taken a pretty girl out on a date. Heck, it'd been a while since he'd dated, period. After the last disaster, he'd sworn off girls. But it got a little lonely sometimes, and he had to admit, when the married guys sat around the table at the station and talked about their wives and lives, it left him with a bit of heavi-

34

ness in his heart. He didn't want to remain single forever. But what was it she had told him? "You have a lot of baggage you need to deal with before you can let me fully in your life." He grumbled at the memory of their last night together and how her words had pierced his heart. It was probably for the best that they'd broken up.

Sam thought a lot about this new face in Dodge City he'd become smitten with. *Smitten, really*? He shook his head and laughed at his choice of words. He reached down and patted his beagle, Charlie, on the head. "She's really cute. Maybe you'll get to meet her."

Dressed in faded blue jeans, a soft-washed tee shirt, and his boots, Sam was as ready as he'd ever be. He didn't like to dress up, and since he wore a uniform to work every day, his closet mainly consisted of jeans in various hues of blue, tee shirts, and well, more tee shirts.

He picked up the dirty clothes that always seemed to miss the hamper, and like a basketball player trying for three points, tossed them into the wicker container. He kicked three pairs of tennis shoes under the bed, ran his hand along the black dresser, moving the dust off and onto the carpet, and pulled up the covers to his bed without really making it. More like just covering the pillows.

He splashed on some cologne that the sales clerk had insisted he buy after she had sprayed a bit in the air and both of them had whiffed it as it wafted through. He hadn't even been in the market for purchasing cologne for himself, but had been aimlessly walking through the fragrance department looking for cologne for *her*. He was sort of glad he hadn't bought her anything; she'd broken up with him that very night, and he'd been single ever since.

He studied his hair in the mirror. "Okay, Miss Lucy girl, here I come, ready or not." Flashing a wide grin in the mirror, he popped his cowboy hat on, adjusting it just so.

As he drove over to her hotel in his pickup truck, he wondered if he'd get a good night kiss. She didn't realize what a brave step he took when he'd introduced himself, or invited her tonight. His breakup had left him a bit uncertain in how to move forward, especially with girls. Normally, he'd have no problem with making the first bold move, but now he was a bit girl shy, and besides, Lucy was different. He wanted to take things slow with her.

He rapped on her hotel door and listened. Soon, he heard light shuffling of shoes on cheap carpet. He relaxed his shoulders as he dug his hands deep into his pockets.

"Hey," she said, smiling ear to ear.

"Hey." His eyes traveled her body, and his heart jumped a bit. She looked gorgeous.

"I'm ready. Just let me grab my purse."

He watched her hips sway gently as she retrieved her purse. When she suddenly turned around, he lifted his eyes to hers.

They walked to the parking lot where old Betsy, his pickup, was parked. Sam opened the passenger door. Lucy's eyes widened at the mess exposed. The seat and floor were covered with straw wrappers, bags from fast-food places, and store receipts.

"Oh, here, let me fix that." He picked up the empty water bottles and tossed them into the back seat. He balled up the zipped-up hoodies, and tossed them back there, too. "There," he said, motioning for her to sit.

She climbed into the seat, straddling a few items at her feet, and then fastened her seat belt.

"Have you ever been to a cattle drive?" He casually looked over at her then put his eyes back on the road.

"No, never." She carefully studied his profile before turning toward the passenger window.

"It's pretty exciting. We have good seats in the stadium. The drive starts at the end of town and they herd them in."

She sprung back around, her eyes widening as she met his stare.

"Don't worry. It's all calculated and monitored. They

won't let those rascals get out of control. Well, not too many of them, anyway." He chuckled.

"Do you dance?" she asked, changing the subject to calm her uneasiness.

"Do I dance?" His eyes sparkled. "I'm one of the best two-steppers in Dodge City." He puffed out his chest.

"Two-step? As in country dancing?"

He nodded. "Don't you know how?"

"No, I'm afraid not. The few times I went out to a club with my friend Beth, we danced to stuff you hear on the top 40 radio stations."

"Well, you're in for a treat, then." He reached over and patted her hand.

She nervously pulled her hand back slightly.

"Here we are. Just let me find a good parking spot," he said, leaning forward and scouting out the lot. "Oh, there," he said, speeding up slightly and turning into a vacant spot.

As they walked, his arm brushed against hers, and then his fingers touched her hand. It would just take a little bit of courage to lace his fingers with hers. His pulse quickened just thinking about making such a move. They found their way to the bleachers and took their seats before he had to make a decision.

"Would you like something to drink?"

"Sure."

"Okay, what would you like?" He gave her a puzzled look.

"Oh, right. I'll have what you're having." She didn't want to make him list everything that was available. Although she would have liked to know everything on the list, she knew it would then take her forever to decide.

"I'll be right back." He stood and then maneuvered his way through the bleachers, taking him out and down to the concession stands.

When he returned, he handed her an ice cold can then he popped the tab on his own and took a big slurp. "Ahh, nothing like a cold beer on a hot day."

She studied the blue and silver can, placing it next to her as she began to dig in her purse.

"Everything okay?" he asked.

"Yes," she said sheepishly as she retrieved a travel-size antibacterial wipe and proceeded to open the foil package. "I just have this thing with germs." She wiped the can down and around the opening where her mouth would go. Satisfied it was sanitary enough, she held the can up to him. "Please pull the tab for me?"

"Are you afraid your fingers will get germs?" He popped the tab.

"No, I just had a manicure." She giggled as she flashed her painted nails at him.

He laughed. "Okay, because I was beginning to

wonder about you Colorado girls." He playfully knocked shoulders with her then turned his attention to the roped off area where the cattle would be crossing through.

He tried to concentrate on the drive, but what really was driving him wild was this pretty little thing with blonde hair and catlike green eyes sitting right next to him. He chugged his beer wondering if she knew how much sensuality she exuded.

All of a sudden, a huge billow of dust appeared, followed by the loud clatter of hooves as the herd passed through the roped off area. He looked over at Lucy to see her expression. Her eyes were as wide as saucers and her back was as stiff as a board. He patted her leg, leaving his hand in place. "Relax. It's safe up here. I've yet to see any of them jump the rope and climb the bleachers," he teased.

She placed her hand above her eyes to shield the sun as she watched. The way she moved her arm, the way she flipped her hair back, and even the way she sipped her beer from the can, moved him. Moved him in more ways than he knew were possible.

"And just like that, it's over." He stood and held out his hand to help her up.

"I'm not finished with my beer yet," she said in protest.

"Bring it."

"WE HAVE some time before the dance starts. I thought I'd take you for a ride."

"Oh, okay. Anywhere in particular?" She smiled.

As usual, she probably overthought what to wear to the barn dance. Lucy sort of liked Sam's scruffy look. In the past, she'd never even give a guy like him a second look, and now she found herself thinking about how it would feel to be wrapped tightly in his arms, how his lips would feel on hers. She casually looked over at him as he drove. Her wild thoughts were insane. How could she even have them? They'd only just met.

He pulled off the main road and traveled down a dusty, gravel road that eventually led them to a secluded area of a lake.

"Isn't this just one of the prettiest places you've ever seen?" He put the truck in park and turned off the engine.

"Well, it is very pretty, but remember … I live in Colorado … Rocky Mountains, lakes, and trails," she said, citing from memory the list of things most people loved about Colorado.

"Yeah, but that's a different kind of pretty. Look how calm that water is," he said, tipping his head toward the lake. "Not even a ripple." He sighed.

"It is very peaceful," she said, agreeing with him.

"We have lakes without ripples, too." Realizing her tone was a bit sarcastic, she followed it with a quirky laugh.

"I brought a blanket." He turned and began to rummage through all the stuff in his back seat, finally producing an olive-green blanket. She wondered when he'd laundered last.

They exited the truck with the blanket, Lucy following close behind him when he suddenly stopped. This is a perfect place. He unrolled the blanket while holding two corners. Lucy quickly picked up the other two giving it a good shake or two. She winced when she caught his mystified look. "I just want to make sure it's free from dust." Still holding the corners securely, the blanket came down after the last shake, hanging in the air like a parachute slowly making its way to landfall.

In silence, they watched a couple of birds dive-bomb the water and then fly off. Something splashed into the water in the distance, causing her to focus to identify what it was.

"A turtle," he said casually.

"Oh, okay. I just didn't want it to be a snake."

"A snake? Do you think a snake would make that kind of splash?" He knocked shoulders with her like he'd done earlier.

"I guess I'm too much of a city girl."

"What happened to Rocky Mountains, trails, and lakes?" He grinned.

"I admit it. I don't get out much. I teach during the days, work on lesson plans in the evenings, and on weekends I usually visit my parents." She shrugged.

"You really should get out more. A pretty girl like you should be out all the time."

His smile bore a hole right through her, causing her heart to beat faster. She quickly rubbed her arms, trying to conceal the goose bumps that had popped up suddenly. "You probably say that to all the girls you bring out here." She tried to sound coy, but the truth of the matter was, she wanted him to kiss her—now.

Just as if he'd read her mind, he moved in, slowly at first studying her. She could see his eyes roaming over her, even though she remained fixed on his. Then he dropped a little closer to her. Her lids slowly closed as she drew in the sweet smell of his warm breath. He tucked a curl behind her ear, and then cupping her face, met her mouth full-on. The kiss started out soft, but soon he devoured her mouth with deep sweeping strokes of his tongue, and she took full advantage of his hungry kiss. It was as if she'd been saving up all her life for this kiss … maybe she had.

CHAPTER 5

"Okay, so just follow my lead. We're going to start off on the right foot with two steps then left foot one step." He held her hands in the dance stance. "Ready?"

Lucy nodded.

He moved her out onto the dance floor. "One, two, one. One, two, one," he repeated over and over as they sashayed around the space. "See? You got it."

"This is fun," she said, keeping time perfectly. He twirled her around, and then as if she'd been dancing two-step all her life, she picked up the timing again and two-stepped around the floor. When the song ended, she pouted playfully. "That was so much fun," she said, beaming at him.

"Told you." He placed his hand on her back and

moved her toward their table. "I say this calls for a drink." He looked over at the large bar that was set up at the other end of the barn. "What can I get for the lady?"

"Something fruity would be lovely."

He quickly kissed her mouth, giving her a little something to remember. "I'll be right back." He winked as he moved away.

He ordered her a fruity cocktail and a scotch, neat, for himself. As the bartender made the drinks, he leaned up against the bar and stared out at the table where he'd left Lucy sitting. He could spot her a mile away. Her blonde hair with the silvery streaks glistened under the little white lights that lit up the barn, and the red shirt she wore made her a guiding light straight to his heart. He recalled their kiss on the blanket, which had left him speechless. And despite her quirky germ thing, he thought she was pretty special and hoped maybe they could get something going. *Oh, who was he kidding?* She was going back to Denver in a few days and he'd probably never see her again.

The closer he got to the table where Lucy sat, the more eager he was to slide his chair closer to hers and sneak a few more kisses in between dancing.

"Here's your drink. He called it *sex on the beach*." He winked as he handed it to her. "Oh, and before you bring out the antibacterial wipes, I saw him wash his hands before he prepared our drinks." He chuckled then slid his chair closer.

"Is my germ phobia that obvious?" She leaned in to the straw and took a sip.

He nodded. "Just a tad. What other phobias do you have besides snakes and germs?" He held the short glass to his lips and breathed in the amber liquor before tasting it.

"Oh, let's see. I'm super OCD. My closet is arranged by shirts, followed by pants, and lastly dresses."

"That doesn't seem too over-the-top."

"Color organized and all the hangers facing the same direction," she added.

"You mean all the blues together and so on?" His eyebrows lifted in anticipation.

She nodded then took another sip of her fruity drink. "This is really good."

"Okay, so you like to be color coordinated. What else?"

"Let's see. My underwear is folded a certain way, and so are my towels. All my spices in the cabinet are arranged by size. I have one shelf for cans, one for boxed food, and in my freezer, I have all meats on one side, veggies on the other. Shall I go on?" She lowered her head in disgust as she heard herself talk.

"Wow, you do have it bad. I know just what will cure

you of all of that." He laughed then took a sip of his scotch.

"Hey, another two-step song, are you ready?" He jumped up and held his hand out.

Lucy stared at him blankly. She shrugged then took his hand.

They sashayed around the floor for another song then the lights dimmed even more as a slow love song began. Sam held her close to his chest, breathing in her warm and fresh scents of whatever it was she bathed in. When she rested her cheek against him, he could feel the warmth of her skin transfer to his own. He bent down and moved his mouth to hers, kissing the softest and juiciest lips he'd ever tasted. She moaned softly, stirring feelings in him that made him wish they were alone. He trailed kisses from her mouth to her neck, causing her to press harder against him, which he so very much liked. He hoped he could maintain his manners and not show his desire for her, but it would be hard to control. He wanted her, and he wanted her now.

IF ONLY HE knew how much she wanted him. This was extreme crazy talk in her view. She'd just met him, for Pete's sake! But something about the way he moved, the way he touched her, and those kisses … that right there was enough for her to abandon all virtue and just do what her heart and body wanted.

"I had a lovely time tonight, Sam," she said, snuggled in his arms up against the truck door.

"Me, too. I don't normally fall for girls this quickly, especially out-of-towners, but you're different. You feel like someone I've known for a long time." He kissed the top of her head as he held her.

"I feel like that, too. It's strange, but when I'm with you, I feel like we're this couple …" she whispered, loving the strength she felt in his arms.

"A couple? Lucy, do you think we could be that? A couple? I'm not just asking so you'll let me make mad love to you. Although, that thought has occurred to me." He held her back and stared at her, making her legs feel all wobbly.

She felt the same way but would never have said it. Well, maybe she would after a few more of those steamy kisses.

"Where do we go from here, Miss Lucy?" He rocked her back and forth in his arms.

"Well, I could invite you up to my room." She leaned back, feeling the warmth of his hold and stared up at him.

"Do you have to spray me down with something first?" He winked.

She hit him on the shoulder. "Sam! This is a real thing I suffer from."

He held her waist and squeezed her. "I know, well, I guess I do. I better read up on it, just so I know what I'm getting myself into." He dropped another kiss on her head.

He moved his mouth to hers and gently eased her mouth open to accept him. She pressed against him, leaving little space while moving her hands around his neck. He slowly stopped the kiss, holding her back. "Let's go," she murmured.

"Let's go to my place," he said, not even trying to end the sweet kisses.

She placed a palm on his chest and stopped him. "Your place?"

"You can meet Charlie." He winked.

"OKAY, now close your eyes. I don't want you to faint," he said with just a touch of teasing in his voice to make her chuckle.

"Why would I faint?"

He led her through the front door. "Keep 'em closed." He moved her toward the sofa. "Okay, you can sit down."

She eased down onto the sofa, still with her eyes

closed. The cushion next to her moved when something or someone pounced near her, startling her. "Sam?"

Sam laughed. "No, that's Charlie. Open your eyes."

She looked to her left to see a large white dog with liver colored spots and a wet tongue hanging out of its mouth. She reached over and patted him. "Hey, there, Charlie."

"Yep, he's my sidekick, aren't you, old Charlie boy?" he said.

She laughed at the baby talk coming from this six-foot-something fireman's mouth. She turned her gaze from him and looked around the room, taking it all in before settling her eyes back on him. "Well, it definitely says a bachelor lives here."

He leaned over and picked up a single white sock that lay on a stack of car magazines. "This is why I said I didn't want you to faint." He smirked then tossed it onto a nearby chair. He settled in next to her on the sofa. "I know I'm not the best organized person, but I'm clean. I take a shower every day, sometimes two, and I brush and floss faithfully after breakfast and dinner." He puffed out his chest as he swung his arm over her shoulders.

"Well, I'm glad to hear your hygiene is in order." She snuggled into him.

"I just don't have many visitors. I live at the station. I

usually work three days then have a day off. Whenever I have a day off, I'm out and about."

"Makes perfect sense to me."

"What I need is a woman's touch." He looked around at the dining table piled high with mail that hadn't yet been sorted, the few dirty dishes in his sink, and the lone white sock looking for its mate.

"That you do, but I might be too much of a woman for you. I mean with my OCD and all." She stayed snuggled in his arms.

"Have you always had OCD?"

"Yep, but they didn't call it that back then. I kept my room pristine, my bathroom was spotless, and well, you already know about my clothes. I always thought that my perfection would cover up my lack of social skills."

"How'd you become a teacher without social skills?" He put his feet up on the coffee table, but quickly removed them when her eyes looked at his feet disapprovingly.

"That's easy. Children are non-judgmental."

"Yeah, but what about their parents?" he asked.

"That can be a bit more challenging, but so far I've had great parents. But there was this one. He was a single dad and he constantly sent his child to school hungry. I finally had to talk to him about it. He first got angry and had me stuttering, but after he settled down and saw that I wasn't a threat to him, we worked it out. He was just trying to do the best he could and he fell a bit short, is all."

"Well, I couldn't be any more opposite of you. I'm messy, unorganized, self-assured to a fault, but somehow, I like how we fit." He kissed her forehead.

"Me, too, but right now everything is new and nice. If we had to live with one another it could be a nightmare—for both of us."

"Maybe, but right now we're just talking about dating. And long distance, at that," he said.

"Long-distance dating never works."

"Who says?" he asked.

"My best friend, Beth."

"What does she know?"

Lucy moved out from his hold and stared at him. "I don't know, but that's what she said."

"Did you tell her about us?"

"Not specifics. It was just in casual conversation."

He stood, now hovering over her. The look in his eyes changed from twinkling to distant.

She reached her hands out to him but he walked away.

"Well, in that case, I guess I better take you back to your hotel. I'd hate for you to waste any more time on a guy who clearly isn't worth dating ... long distance, that is." He picked up his keys from the table and jangled them.

She didn't have a clue what he'd been through regarding women, but one thing was for sure, Sam Lyons didn't have time for games. She stood and grabbed her purse and moved to the front door. "Okay, then." She turned the knob.

"Okay, then." He closed the door behind them.

After an agonizingly silent trip, they finally arrived at the hotel. She didn't even wait for him, instead, she jumped right out of the truck and made her way toward her hotel room.

He popped open his door and slipped out. "So, just like that, huh?" he yelled.

She whirled around. "Well, it seems that's what you wanted all along—an easy breakup. You cowboys are all alike."

He chewed on his bottom lip. One thing firemen never wanted to be called was a cowboy. "Get it right. I'm a fireman, not a cowboy," he yelled, shaking his head.

"Whatever." She stormed down the sidewalk to her door.

"Lucy Carmichael, don't walk away from me," he yelled.

"Sam Lyons, leave me alone," she called back. "I wish I'd never laid eyes on you."

He ripped off his hat and flipped it inside the truck and then slammed the door, running to catch her before she went inside. Breathing heavily from running, he pulled her arm back just as she was about to insert her key.

Tears fell from her eyes and she began to cry.

"Lucy, don't." His chest rose and fell as he tried to catch his breath.

"How did this happen? We were having a great time and now we're fighting like mad dogs." She cupped her face and sobbed.

He pulled her hands down and held them in his. "I'm sorry. I think I got angry because your friend said we didn't have a chance. She doesn't even know us. We're good together, Lucy." His soft voice made her take notice.

"You're right. I shouldn't have listened to her. I don't think I really believed her, but I—"

He stopped her with a kiss. She reached up and laced her hands around his neck, holding him in place.

He took the key out of her hand, and while still kissing her, unlocked the door, letting them both in. He kicked the door shut, his lips never leaving hers.

She moved away from him, holding his hands. "You know what this means, don't you?"

He studied her face with the most serious of looks then shook his head.

With hands on her hips and squinting eyes she said, "You have anger issues on top of being messy and unorganized."

His deer in the headlight look made it difficult to maintain her smug grin. She went into a full smile that turned into severe laughter that resulted in her snorting as she grabbed her sides.

"And you, Miss Lucy, are a prankster. Just you wait," he said, picking her up and twirling her around. He held her and then let her gently glide through his hands, putting her feet firmly on the floor. "And it's that sort of thing that draws me to you." He moved his hands to her waist and held her tightly.

"Even when I snort like a little pig?" She flashed a wide grin.

"It just shows you're not perfect and that's okay. I like you for all of your little nuances, good and bad."

"That's just a nice way of saying faults, you know." She leaned back into his hold, staring at him hard. She'd never stared at anyone so hard in her life. Not even the worst kid in her class.

"Faults, nuances. I say character. You have a lot of character." He pulled her in closer.

"Sam, you know I go back to Denver the day after tomorrow." Her tone shifted, and now what was once a funny moment, turned serious.

"I know, babe, but let's make the most of it. Tomorrow is the rodeo. And then after that," he bent down and gave her a quick kiss, "I thought we could go out to the lake." He kissed her again as he swung her back and forth.

"Okay, but I'm going to cry when we say goodbye. I'm just warning you now." Her eyes filled with mist.

"Aww, honey, don't cry. We haven't said goodbye, yet." He pulled her in for a hug.

She said something but her voice was muffled by his tight hold on her against his chest.

"What?" He held her back, tilting his ear to hear her better. "I couldn't understand what you were saying."

"I just said I'm finding out I'm less perfect every second I'm with you." She choked out a lighthearted laugh.

"Perfection is in the eye of the beholder. And you … are perfect for me."

CHAPTER 6

The loud music got his adrenaline going, and soon he was thumping his fingers to the beat as he gripped the steering wheel. *Can this really be happening? The guys back at the firehouse are going to tease me unmercifully.* "I don't really care if they do." His mind always went back to her soft lips, warm cheeks, and sensual touch.

He'd had his share of love 'em and leave 'em in his twenty plus years. It was hard to have a lasting relationship with his crazy schedule. It would always start out great, just like it was with Lucy, and then slowly erode over time because of jealousy issues, not spending enough quality time together, and then there were his mother/father issues that sometimes waltzed into his relationships, and never at an opportune time. His baggage.

He tried hard to not be the man his father was, but every now and again, a blast from the past entered his mind, and he wondered if he was good enough for the current love of his life. The guys at the station would tell him he loved hard and easy, but it always came down to the women in his life just couldn't love his job as much as they loved him.

He had a lot of respect for both his mother and sister, although his mom had to really earn it. She went from one bad relationship to another. She just couldn't see it. He recalled the day he'd let her have it. He'd asked her why she liked being used as a doormat, why she liked to be a kept woman, not free to think or do for herself. He knew he'd never be attracted to a woman who felt she was less than capable of making her own decisions. Sure, he was a little bit old school deep in his soul. He liked to open doors for women, pay for the date, compliment her in every way he could think, bring her flowers, and hold her tight when she was scared. But he also liked women who were bold enough to make the first move, not be afraid of their sensuality, or hold him when he was scared. He had plenty to fear, too, rejection being on the top of the list.

Lucy pulled up her long golden locks into a ponytail and secured it with a rubber band. She inserted her new earrings she'd purchased at the crafts show; they were one of her favorite gems, emerald. They weren't really emeralds, but the vivid green color set her eyes off just right, and she liked the way they looked on her, especially with her yellow and green plaid shirt. She rolled up the sleeves and secured them with the button tabs and tucked it into her slim fitting jeans. Being from Colorado, boots were the norm, and although she didn't wear them often, she did own a pair. She stood back and admired her look in the wall-to-wall mirror over the sink. She stood back farther so she could get a better glimpse of the entire outfit. Never quite satisfied with her look, she sighed and then with a flip of her ponytail, turned and took a seat while waiting for Sam.

Pulling open the door, she greeted him with a smile first then a kiss. With a smile she stepped back, letting her eyes float to his blue button-down shirt with just the cuffs folded back and showing off his strong hands and forearms. His jeans fit in all the right places, showing off his assets to a tee.

"Well, well, well," he said, shaking his head as he checked her out.

She could feel the heat rising to her cheeks, and held

up her hand. "Stop. You're going to make me blush. Besides, I was just going to compliment you."

"Too late for that. Your cheeks are red like tomatoes on a vine."

She batted her lashes. "Like tomatoes on a vine, huh? That's a new one." She reached for her purse and sweater that hung over the chair. "I'm ready to see the rodeo," she chimed.

He motioned her to go first and then they headed out.

THE EXCITEMENT at the rodeo was super intense. Crowds of people filled the stands in anticipation of a great show.

"So, you say you've never been to a rodeo before?" He knitted his brows as he tried to make sense of this.

She didn't want to admit it, but it was the truth. "I know it seems weird, but I just don't—"

He cut her short. "Get out much." He leaned into her shoulder and then dropped a kiss right on top of it.

She lifted her shoulders and sighed.

"Well, that's all gonna change now that you're with me. We're gonna do and see everything we can because we only have this one life here on earth, ya know?"

"I agree. I want to. It's just that I'm so awkward when I get around a large crowd, unless it's children."

"I know this is probably not the place to talk about it, but do you know why you have some of these feelings? Have you ever talked to a professional about them?"

She shook her head adamantly. "No, never. I have to be careful because there's a stigma attached to seeking professional help. I don't want to lose my job."

"That's crazy! Well, maybe I can help you."

"You'd do that for me?" She blinked back a tear that tried to make an appearance.

"I told you, Lucy, you're very important to me. If I can help in any way, I will. As a fireman, we are told all the time that if we need to talk to a professional, we can. I think if you want to see one here, I can arrange it. Denver would never have to know."

Lucy didn't take her eyes off the arena for the entire rodeo. The rush she felt from all the excitement made her feel like a kid who had eaten an entire bag of candy. When Sam asked her what her favorite event was she couldn't decide.

"I enjoyed the skill the bronc riders had. They had to stay on there for eight seconds and they couldn't touch the horse with their free hand. That takes a lot of practice."

"Yep, and when they fall, it hurts." He chuckled.

"I also enjoyed the timed events. But are you sure the calves and goats don't get hurt at all?" She lowered her head and peered at him above her sunglasses.

He laughed. "I promise. No animals were hurt in the making of this rodeo."

She laughed at the parody of equating rodeos with commercials. "Barrel racing was intense," she continued. "But I think the kid events were so special, especially the stick pony race. Weren't they just adorable?"

"Those are future rodeo contesters," he said.

They held hands as they made their way to his truck. He helped her in and then shut her door. After he settled into the driver's seat, he angled his body toward her. With one hand on the steering wheel, he reached for her with his free hand. She placed her hand in his.

After letting out a rush of air, he spoke. "I can't believe our time together is about to come to an end." He made circles on her thumb with his.

"I know," she whispered.

"I've had a great ten days with you, Miss Lucy Carmichael. I hope I did justice to Dodge City." He squeezed her hand.

A small coy laugh escaped her lips. "You could say that," she said, her eyes blooming with desire.

He let go of her hand and started the engine. "Lake?" He locked gazes with her.

She nodded.

THE GLOW from the moon shimmered across the sheet-glass like surface of the lake, and night bugs serenaded them. Every now and then Lucy could hear a light rustling through the tall weeds, but for once in her life, she stayed calm. Being enveloped in his strong arms had that effect on her. That and the battery-operated lantern he'd brought along.

She drank in all the smells of him and their surroundings, and she didn't want to move a muscle. "I could stay here like this all night," she said, staring up at the moon.

"It is nice out here, isn't it?" He reached up and gently tugged at her ponytail. "Do you mind?" He started to release her hair.

"No," she whispered.

He pulled her hair loose from the rubber band and let it fall around her shoulders. He ran his fingers through it, tucking some strands behind her ears. "You're so beautiful. I can't stop saying it." He leaned in and kissed her.

If he only knew how much he stirred feelings inside her. She wondered if she'd ever be able to tell him …

show him how much she felt for him. Her experiences with men were few and far between, and although her dad turned his life around and became the father and husband he was today, Lucy recalled some difficult times, and sometimes it's hard to leave the past in the past.

Sam reached over and picked a tall thick reed and began to chew on it. "You never talk about your parents."

She gasped. It was as if he'd read her mind. She pulled out of his hold and turned toward him. "I was just thinking about them."

"Oh, yeah?" He tossed the reed he'd been chewing on out toward the lake.

"My dad wasn't always father of the year." There, she said it.

"Mine either."

Her eyes widened. "He drank excessively and then they'd fight. I stayed in my room a lot, and as a result, never had too many friends. I just didn't know when he'd be drunk or when a fight would break out." She was amazed how easily the truth came out.

"I have a similar story, but it doesn't end well. My dad drank himself to death, and my mother ended up marrying some guy who hit her all the time. So, she went from living with a drunk to living with an abusive man." He reached over and grabbed another tall reed.

"That's awful, Sam." She ran her hand along his forearm, trying to soothe his pain away. "Was Wanda living there at that time?"

"No, she moved out when she was seventeen. I had to make sure she finished high school and then enrolled in a tourism program at the local junior college. She's doing well. She doesn't really have a great relationship with Mom, but they're working on it."

She leaned back on her arms. "Dysfunctional families —it's a wonder we turned out so well."

"I'm okay. I learned," he leaned in and looked right at her, "that by talking to a shrink, you can't fix some stuff. Some of it is on the other person. I finally told my mom that if she wanted to live with a guy who thought she was worthy of punches to the face, then that was on her. But if she wanted help to escape the situation, I'd be here." He plucked another dry reed turning it over and over in his fingers.

"My dad cleaned up his act because he finally saw the light. He and Mom started going to church, and before I knew it, the liquor cabinet was void of all alcohol and they began to heal." She drew back, her eyes wide with surprise when he slapped his leg.

"Sorry, I didn't mean to startle you. My mom had a similar occurrence. The neighbor in the apartment below her invited her to church. He didn't want her to go, but she did it anyway. They convinced her to let us all help her get out of that situation. I'm happy to say she's now living alone—except for the dog that I got her, and she's doing well. But, boy, was it a tough climb getting there." He shook his head.

"Do you go to church?" she asked.

"No, but that doesn't mean that I don't believe. I'm just busy. I work a lot, and well, we do pray during team meals and after we return from a fire or hairy situation. I said one the night of the hotel fire when I met you." His smile warmed her heart.

"I don't either, but I do pray."

He reached over and took her hands in his. "I know we just met, and I don't want to come on too strongly, but Lucy, what I feel for you is so intense. I just don't know how I'll handle it when you're gone."

"You'll handle it just fine, just like I will. That's what we have to do. Denver is only a six-hour drive. I'll visit, and maybe you can come see me? I'd love for you to meet my parents."

"Okay, but right now we have tonight." He pulled her close, his lips just mere centimeters from hers. She could feel the warmth of his breath as he held her. He lowered his face closer, and when his lips touched hers, she melted into him.

They must have said goodbye fifty times, and in just as many ways. He'd kiss her then hold her tightly, she'd start to say goodbye then he'd pull her in for another long kiss. This went on for about fifteen minutes when she finally said she better get on the road.

"I want to get home before dark," she pleaded as he trailed kisses down her neck.

"I just can't let you go," he murmured.

"I'll be back, soon. I promise." She drew in her bottom lip as his mouth traveled to hers.

A soft moan escaped her mouth when he pressed another kiss to her lips. Shaking her head, she heaved a big sigh. He started to move in again, cupping her face with his big strong hands, but this time, she placed her palm on his chest so he couldn't complete his mission. She was already feeling very vulnerable about their whole sad situation. "Sam, this is not helping me leave." A tear rolled down her cheek.

He dropped his hands, giving up the fight, and reached for her car door. He opened it wide and then rested his hands on the top of the door frame. She could feel his eyes on her as she got in, and she should have known better than to look right then. His eyes beckoned her to stay but she knew she had to go. She had to prepare her classroom for the new school year, go shopping for new clothes, and then there was her family's annual week getaway celebrating the anniversary of their new beginning as a healthy family.

She started the engine. He slammed the door shut and waited for her to roll down the window. "I'll be back." She moistened her dry mouth.

He leaned into the open window and kissed her, before stepping back to watch her drive away. He didn't know it, but he'd just taken a piece of her heart, leaving a gaping hole the size of Kansas.

He watched her until he couldn't see her anymore, then hung his head and kicked a couple of nearby stones, just because. Digging his hands deep into his pockets, he squinted toward the cloudless blue sky. He knew better than to put his heart out on his sleeve. Hadn't he learned you can't do that, especially with someone who didn't even live here? He moseyed over to his truck and got inside. His bereft soul, now void of Lucy's joy, left him feeling like someone had just died.

CHAPTER 8

"How was Idaho?" Lucy held the phone to her ear as she unpacked.

"Exciting," Beth exclaimed loudly, causing Lucy to hold the phone away from her ear.

"Not boring Idaho this time?"

"I met someone."

"Really?" Lucy sat on the edge of her bed. "So did I."

"You tell me about your guy first."

"He's the one I told you about. Remember there was a fire at the hotel where I was staying? I got woken up in the middle of the night—"

"Lucy, what's that got to do with your guy?" Beth said, cutting her off.

"Let me finish. Anyway, there I was, standing out in

the dark parking lot in my camisole and shorts with a sweater on, when I spotted the most gorgeous eyes poking out from under a fireman's hat."

"You never flirt. This is new."

"I didn't flirt," Lucy protested. "Well, I sort of did," she said, thinking back on her lame one-liner to get him to notice her. "Later, I ran into him after the car show during my lunch, and then I saw him at the parade, and then we ran into each other yet again … it just ballooned into something. It's crazy." She lowered her back onto the bed and stared at the ceiling. "I think I love him, and I know how silly that sounds."

"It's not silly, but you know how hard a long distant relationship will be, right?"

Lucy sighed. "I do. Tell me about your guy."

"Well, it was an old high school flame of mine. I sort of forgot about him because, really, he wasn't that impor-tant to me. We went on a couple of dates and to the prom together. But holy cow, did he turn into one handsome man. I couldn't take my eyes off of him, and well, as you said, it ballooned into something. And yes, it is crazy." She spoke a mile a minute, causing Lucy's mind to race along with her friend's words.

Lucy stayed silent for a moment, taking it all in.

"Lucy, are you there?"

"Yes, I'm here. I was just thinking about the coincidence of our two vacations." Wondering if her friend had changed her tune regarding long-distance dating, she asked, "Are you going to date long distance?"

"Yes, we're going to try, but truthfully, I'm thinking about applying for some teaching jobs back home. My parents are ecstatic about me coming home, too."

Lucy popped up from her prone position. "Transfer to Idaho?"

"I know, but it's not that far away. You can come visit me on your next adventure."

"True." Lucy stood and grabbed her dirty clothes bag from her suitcase and loosened the drawstring that kept it closed.

"Let's get together for dinner and talk more about it," Beth said.

"Sounds good. I have dinner plans over at the folks' tomorrow. We're going over our family vacation plans."

"Oh, right, the annual we're a happy family again trip," Beth quipped.

"Yep, that one." Lucy dumped her dirty clothes into her pink laundry basket.

"Okay, my friend, talk to you soon. Right now I have to get on the computer and look for teaching jobs. Now is the time most districts are filling vacancies."

"Okay, and right now I have lots of laundry to do. Your plans sound a bit more fun."

"Ha ha. Talk to you later. Bye."

"Bye." Lucy stuck the phone in her pocket, grabbed some change off of her dresser, and picked up her laundry basket.

NO MISSED CALLS or messages from Sam for two days. He must be busy. She looked at her phone for a long time before tossing it on the coffee table. She began flipping through channels to find something to occupy her mind and keep the negative thoughts out. She had to keep reminding herself that he was a fireman. He worked long hours. He had another life in Dodge City. Her heart ached to hear his voice, yet she was too insecure to call him. What if he didn't really have the deep feelings for her that she had for him? Maybe he was just playing with her. She slumped back onto the sofa cushion and sighed.

Her phone startled her when it began ringing. Hopeful it was Sam, her spirits soon dropped when she realized it was her mom.

"What time are you coming over—" her mother asked.

Lucy gasped. She'd been concentrating so hard on Sam and why he hadn't called that she'd totally forgotten about family night. "Oh, Mom, sorry! I'll be right over," she said, hanging up the phone, cutting her mom off in mid-sentence. She turned off the television and grabbed her purse. This was so unlike her to forget an appointment. *What is happening?*

She drove quickly, worried that her parents would be disappointed in her lateness. Now, that was more like the old Lucy, always worried about what others thought. She picked up her speed, and then she heard a siren start up. Looking in her rearview mirror, she discovered a motor-cycle cop behind her flashing his lights. She pulled over.

"I'm sorry, Officer. I was trying to get to my parents'," she blurted.

"Driver's license and registration, please."

She dug in her glove box and retrieved the registra-tion and handed it to him. While he looked it over, she produced her driver's license.

"I'll be right back." He headed back to his bike.

She shook like a scared rabbit, chewing on her finger-nails while she waited. Her stomach felt like it was doing backflips and a wave of nausea washed over her. Soon the policeman returned and handed over her documents.

"I'm going to let you off with a warning this time, but if I catch you speeding like you're trying to get to a fire again, I'm going to write you a ticket."

Fire. Sam. "Yes, sir. I won't. Thank you."

She drove under the speed limit all the way to her parents' house and felt a moment of relief when she finally pulled into their driveway. But now she had to explain why she had forgotten about their dinner.

"Okay, before you say anything," she said, holding up a hand, "I forgot about our dinner tonight because I've had a lot of things on my mind lately."

Marjorie looked over at Paul then back at her daughter. "Dinner plans for tonight?"

Lucy widened her eyes. She pulled out her phone and looked at her calendar. She tossed her head back. "Oh, man!"

"Tomorrow night," Marjorie said. "You didn't even give me a chance to confirm. As soon as I asked you what time you were coming over, you blasted me with I'm coming right now and hung up the phone. I tried to call you back but your phone went straight to voice mail."

Lucy looked back at her screen. *Missed call. Voice message.* "I got pulled over for speeding. My phone was silenced. Sorry."

Paul stepped toward Lucy and moved his hand up and down her arm. "Everything okay with my little girl?" His eyes twinkled when he spoke.

"We can move dinner up to tonight. I know I have

something I can pull together really fast," Marjorie said, realizing they might be in crisis mode regarding Lucy.

She blinked back the first few tears, trying to hold them back but they weren't listening, and neither was the steady stream of them standing by. She finally cupped her hands and sobbed into them.

"Order pizza, Marjorie," Paul said, leading Lucy into the other room.

Marjorie took off for the phone while Paul and Lucy sat down in the family room. "What's going on?" He lifted her chin with his finger. "This is not like you. What happened in Kansas?"

A father always knew, right? Or was it a mother always knew? At any rate, Paul knew. "I had the time of my life in Dodge City, that's what happened." She looked at his face for comfort.

Paul drew in a deep breath and let it out slowly. "You met someone?"

She nodded.

"Pizza is on the way," Marjorie said, plopping down in a nearby chair.

"Mom, I think I'm in love." This revelation even startled Lucy. *Where did that outburst come from? From deep inside, where apparently the truth can never stay hidden for long.*

Marjorie clasped her hands in her lap and blinked. "In

love? I thought you were going to the rodeo … Oh." She stopped suddenly, adding two and two.

"Not one of the rodeo cowboys," Lucy clarified. "A fireman."

"A fireman?" Paul said.

"Remember when I told you about the evacuation of the hotel? Well, one of the firemen on duty that night."

"I guess Dodge City is a small town." Marjorie sat back in her chair and crossed her legs.

"It's not that small, but yes, it does have a small-town charm. I really liked it there. But now, I don't know if he really feels the same way. I haven't gotten a phone call from him and it's been two days since I got back." She began to pick at the frayed nail she'd chewed earlier.

"Okay, so let's put this into perspective," Paul said. "He's a fireman. Firemen are busy. It's summertime, with lots of heat and fires. Let's give him … what's his name?"

"Sam."

"Let's give Sam the benefit of the doubt. If you don't hear from him by tomorrow, call him. This is 2018. It's okay to call guys, right, Marjorie?" Paul looked to his wife for confirmation.

"Yes, by all means," Marjorie said, agreeing with her husband.

"Now, let's talk about our family vacation and get our minds onto happier things," Paul said.

Over pepperoni slices and frosty root beer, the Carmichaels went over the plans for their vacation. Paul was so excited about renting a motor home. A week with the three of them cooped up in a camper didn't sound like much fun to Lucy, but then Paul unfolded the brochures and they mapped out trails to hike, discussed what food to bring, where they would take dips to cool off in nearby lakes, and the nightly bonfire and roasting of marshmallows. It began to sound like a great trip. One she wished she could share with Sam.

After they discussed the vacation and filled up on pizza and root beer, Lucy announced that she was going home. She crossed over to the front door, her legs feeling like heavy weights were tethered around them.

"Try to get some sleep, hon. It'll all work out, you'll see." Paul always knew what to say to bring a smile to her face.

"Now drive home safely," Marjorie said.

"Yep, no speeding tickets," her dad quipped.

"I got a warning," she reminded them.

Paul laughed. "Good night, dear. Call us tomorrow after you hear from your fellow." He waved from the front stoop.

"Yes, dear, keep the faith. But if he doesn't call, do

what your dad said. Call him. He's probably just busy." She flashed a smile Lucy could see even in the dark.

Lucy lifted her hand in a wave and then got into her car.

SHE TRIED to read a few pages in her book but her mind kept wandering to Sam and how he could be so cruel after taking a piece of her heart. She thought their feelings were mutual and this is how he reciprocated, by not reaching out or following up. He didn't even know if she'd made it home safely.

She tossed the book onto the nightstand and picked up her phone. *Should she do it?* She shook her head, and then lightly tapping her head a few times against the oak headboard, dialed his number.

"You've reached Sam. I can't talk right now. I'm fighting a fire or something. Leave your name and number and I'll call you when I can."

Lucy listened to the beep then hung up. Tears welled up and soon trailed down her face. She slipped under the covers and cried herself to sleep.

BETH AND LUCY managed to squeeze in a lunch just before she hit the road in the motor home with her parents. She wasn't as excited about the lunch anymore since she hadn't heard from Sam. *What would she tell her friend? That apparently her feelings all had been one-sided?*

She arrived at the restaurant before Beth, got a table, and began looking over the menu while she waited. After a few minutes, her bubbly friend walked in.

"Hey, how are you?" Her eyes sparkled like she was madly in love.

"Great. You look great, too," Lucy said, admiring her rosy cheeks—another sign of being in love.

"I just got off the phone with Caleb." She flashed a grin and then picked up the menu.

Instead of looking at lunch options, Lucy focused on Beth as she studied the menu.

When Beth made her selection, she let the menu slide down, her eyes locking with Lucy's. "Everything okay with you? You seem a bit different." Beth's expression softened as she waited for her response.

Lucy lowered her gaze.

"Lucy Carmichael, I know when something is wrong, and something is definitely wrong."

Her watery eyes gave it away.

"Aww, hon, what's up? Is it the cowboy?"

"He's not a cowboy," she said, her voice muffled.

"He didn't call?"

Her eyes flashed up to Beth. "How'd you know that?"

"That's the *he didn't call* look right there," she said, tipping her head toward Lucy.

"Yeah, I don't know what happened. He practically begged me not to go, and now that I'm here, he doesn't even call me." She shook her head in disgust.

"Maybe something happened to him. Did you try calling him?"

"Yeah, but his voice mail answered so I hung up."

"Hung up? That's crazy. Everyone has voice mail. Maybe he was out fighting a fire."

Lucy laughed.

"What's so funny?"

Lucy shook her head. She didn't want to take the time to explain about his voice mail greeting.

"Call him, Lucy!"

"I might tonight. I just thought he'd be burning up the lines calling me."

"I know you and you don't jump into relationships. That's just not your MO. You're a great judge of character, too. So, I say something is up. Maybe he had an appendicitis attack and is in the hospital recuperating from surgery."

Lucy conjured up images in her mind of him lying in

a ditch somewhere, or under bright lights in a surgical clinic. She drew in her bottom lip and began to twirl a strand of hair. "I'm really worried."

"Well, just call him. Can I tell you about Caleb, or is that like rubbing salt in an open wound right now?"

Lucy smiled. "No, tell me. I want to feel happy about something."

CHAPTER 9

*L*ucy was happy for her friend's love life, and made sure she showed how supportive she could be, even when her own love life was falling apart right before her eyes, if she'd even had one, to begin with. "I'm really happy that you've found Caleb." Lucy's eyes glistened with just a touch of moisture as she tried to sound convincing.

Standing near their parked cars, Lucy looked off into the distance to give her eyes a chance to dry out. When she turned back toward Beth, she had every intention of speaking, but when she hesitated, her friend reasoned with her.

"Listen, Lucy … I know things are going to work out for you guys. Everything you told me about him seems too perfect. Something has happened. I know you're scared of rejection, but you must call and leave a message. It's the only way you'll know for sure."

"I know."

"Do it today. Call me later." Beth unlocked her door.

Leaning up against her own car door, Lucy watched as her friend drove away. She climbed into the driver's seat and started the engine, cranking up her radio. She'd driven about two blocks when her phone began to ring. She looked over at the screen. She gasped and then tried to find a place to pull over. It was Sam. "Sam, wait, I'm here. Don't hang up," she pleaded as she cut across lanes, almost causing an accident.

It was too late. He'd hung up. But wait! There was a message. She hit the message button and listened.

"Hey, Lucy. I know I haven't called and you're probably worried sick about me. I'm okay, but the team and I have been fighting a huge fire outside of the city. It's made national news so I'm sure you've heard about it. I haven't had any cell coverage or I would have called sooner. Back in town to get some supplies and then back out to the fire. Anyway, I'm safe, but will be out of reach for a few more days until relief firefighters get here. I miss you. Talk to you soon."

She slammed her head against the headrest of her seat. "*Grr!* I'm such an idiot. I feel awful for thinking the worst. My Sam ... he really does care." A smile formed across her lips and then a few tears of joy trailed down her face.

She dialed Beth's number.

"Hey, Lucy."

"He cares. He just called."

"Just now?"

"I missed it. I was driving, but he left a message. You were right. He's been fighting a fire for days out on the edge of town. He said it made the national news. I haven't been watching the news, though. I feel like a complete idiot."

"No, don't be so hard on yourself. I'm just glad he called."

"Beth?"

"Uh-huh?"

"Thanks for being my friend. I wish you a lot of luck and much happiness in Idaho with Caleb. I can't wait to meet the guy who stole my best friend's heart. I'm going to miss you like crazy, but I think you're doing the right thing." This time, she said it like she really meant it.

"Thanks, Lucy. Talk soon."

Lucy drove home in a daze. She gathered her thoughts about what she'd say on her return message to Sam. She knew he wouldn't hear it for a few days, but she had to say something.

But first she called her mother. "He called!"

"Oh, good, dear. Now we can stop worrying."

"You were worrying? Why were you worrying?"

"Because we don't like to see our little girl sad and unhappy," Marjorie said.

Lucy shook her head. Boy, did she lay it on thick. "Mother, first of all, I'm not a little girl, although I may have acted like it the last few days. But I feel better, and if anything, this little test of faith has me on the path to something bigger."

"Oh?"

"I feel this weight lifted from my shoulders, bringing me calmness and serenity, but also I feel a bit more confident now. I just needed assurance from Sam that he cared. I should have known it all along, but this is something I'm overcoming. I still have some major hang-ups from that dark time in our lives."

"That's great, dear. I'm glad you're feeling better. I still have periods of doubt, but you know who I trust, right?"

Lucy knew she meant God.

"I'm ready for this vacation, how about you?" Marjorie shouted into the phone.

"Yes, I'm so ready."

~

LUCY LEFT a reply message to Sam's. She kept it brief but let him know she missed him as well and looked forward to when they could talk a long time. She left off any words that might have even hinted at her insecurities. He didn't need that right now, especially when he was fighting a major fire.

The family vacation went well, and except for a sprained ankle that Paul got from stepping on a stone and landing wrong during one of their hikes, and some bug bites they all received, the trip was a success. Oh, and then there was the dent in the bumper that no one wanted to talk about, least of all Lucy.

"Well, if you hadn't sprained your ankle I wouldn't have had to drive that boat home," Lucy said, eyeing the dent.

Paul grumbled under his breath.

"I'm sorry, Dad. I just misjudged how close I was."

"It's okay. It's why we have insurance." He shrugged.

She looped her arms around his waist and snuggled into her dad's arms. "I had a great time, though. It was probably our best family vacation ever." She looked up at her dad.

"I agree. Where should we go next year?"

"Oh, I don't know, maybe Dodge City?" She grinned.

She kept telling her parents she wasn't a little girl. She was twenty-five years old, anything but a little girl.

But sometimes, when she was in her dad's arms, twirling the soft grey hair on his forearms, she still felt like a little girl. It reminded her of the good days.

"Dodge City sounds like a fine place for a family vacation." He dropped a kiss on her forehead.

LUCY HAD JUST MADE a cup of tea and sat down, leafing through a magazine, when Sam called. She'd practiced how she'd greet him, aiming to not sound too excited, but when she heard his voice on the other end, all bets were off regarding cool, calm, and collected Lucy Carmichael.

"Sam! How are you? I've been so scared about your safety." She held the phone tightly against her ear. The static in the background made it difficult to hear him clearly.

"I'm good. I miss you, babe. I'm traveling back to the city and as soon as I had cell coverage I wanted to call you."

"Are the fires contained?"

"Just about—it's burned over forty thousand acres."

"I saw it on the news." She didn't have the heart to tell him that she hadn't watched until after she'd heard his message. "It is devastating. Do they know the cause of the fire?"

"No, but they suspect arson."

"I'm just glad you're safe. I saw some of the fire-fighters were treated for burns."

"It's a dangerous job, Lucy, but I love what I do."

The reception crackled in her ear.

"Hello?" Sam said.

"I'm here," Lucy said, thinking about his last statement.

"Sam, what are we going to do?"

"Do about what?"

"Us. I'm so lost without you." There, she said it.

"I knew it would be hard having a long-distance thing, but I guess I didn't know how hard."

She gulped. "Do you think we should still try?" Her heart pounded in her chest. There was a long silence and she wasn't sure if they were still connected. Her throat tightened. "Sam? Do you still want to try?" The pulsating kicked up a notch, pounding louder in her ears.

"I do, but I don't know how it's going to work out. I mean, I know being intimate is not everything to a relationship, but—"

She didn't allow him to finish. "I know. You have needs." She'd just stop beating around the bush and say what he was feeling, although she hoped she was wrong. Surely their relationship was more than just sex?

"Yes, and I think you do, too. At least you showed me

you do." His sexiness came through the phone and had the heat building up all through her body in five seconds. She reached up and touched her face. It burned with passion. *He was right. Of course, he was.*

"Yes, I do, but it's because of you, Sam. I don't have a lot of experience with men. I told you that. You do something to me that I can't explain, but I'll understand if it's too much to continue with our relationship. I won't lie —I'll be sad, and I might even cry over you." *Heck, who was she fooling? She'd sob over the breakup.* "But I won't be hanging on to you if that's not what you want."

"Let's try for a bit longer, but I want you to know, I did care about you. I *do* care about you. I just think it was too quick. We didn't really get a chance to be together before you left. We don't have anything built up. It's all new. You know what I mean?"

He made perfect sense, but at the same time, she added, "I get it, but we do have a little something we can build on, right? Maybe we don't have an established rela-tionship, or past, but what we do have is a lot of chem-istry, and I'm willing to hang in there with you, if that's what you want." She felt better getting it out in the open that she wasn't throwing in the towel just yet.

"Okay, I'm going to be off for the next five days—a little R & R after the fires. How about I drive up to Denver?"

Her eyes lit up. "Yes! That will be great. I can't wait to see you."

"I can't wait to wrap my arms around you and kiss your sweet lips."

His hunger came through the line, loud and clear.

A secret smile emerged on her lips. "I'll be ready," she said with a ring of sexiness she didn't know she had.

CHAPTER 10

ucy pushed her shopping cart up and down the aisles of her local super store, looking for unique things as well as the required supplies to furnish her classroom. She stopped in front of the colored pencils and tossed in several packages. It seemed every year there were a few students who didn't have the required supplies. She made it her mission that no child would feel left out. She tossed in several tubes of glitter, and then headed to the pet section. Lucy was particularly excited about this year's classroom project—designing terrariums using fishbowls. She picked up a bag of colorful rocks. Pulling her brows together in serious contemplation, she tapped her finger to her mouth as she quickly tried to calculate how many she'd need. Grabbing four bags, she tossed them into the cart. Satisfied she'd made a decent dent in her first of many shopping trips before and during the school year, she made her way toward the registers to pay.

SHE'D JUST GATHERED her bags when her phone rang. Why is it when you have your hands full either your nose itches or your cell phone deep inside your pocket or purse begins to ring? Shaking her head, she let the bags roll off of her hands and wrists, then began digging in her purse to retrieve her phone.

"Hey," she said, her eyes lighting up when she heard his voice.

"How are you?"

"Just fine now that I heard your voice." She leaned over and threaded the handles of the plastic bags through her free arm and grabbed her purse.

"I'm just heading out now," he said.

She wanted to look at the time but she didn't want to move the phone from her ear. "What time is it, anyway?"

"It's about noon. I got a late start—had a few loose ends, but I'll be there by dinnertime."

Dinner. In her foggy state of mind she'd totally forgotten to set up dinner with her folks. "Ah, shoot. I forgot to set something up with my parents. Maybe we can just eat in tonight and I'll work out something for tomorrow."

"Well, about that. Something has come up and I have to cut my trip short. I'll just be staying for the one night. Maybe I can meet them another time?"

She let the purse and bags slide off her arm. The silence between them was obvious. "Why?" She calmed her voice, trying to remain positive.

"I'm going to help a buddy out. Work his shift so he can take his wife out for their anniversary."

"That's very nice of you, but couldn't someone else do it? I mean, you said they gave you a few days off because of all the hours you put in. I was looking forward to spending some time with you … introducing you to my parents, showing you around. Maybe you should wait and come another time when you can stay longer." She hated to sound like a whiney girlfriend, but she really wanted to see him. If he only knew how many sleepless nights she'd had thinking about him and wishing he was with her, with his loving arms wrapped around her.

"I know you're disappointed. I'll make it up to you." His sexy swagger waltzed right in through the phone, making her knees buckle.

"I guess," she said, sounding again like the whiney, righteous girlfriend she didn't want to be.

"Lucy, I told you before that my job is very important. The guys I work with are like family. If they need something, I'm there for them. I hope you understand that." Now he was sounding a bit condescending and it made her feathers ruffle just a tad. He didn't really need to go there, did he?

"I know it's important to you. I was hoping I was up there somewhere on the totem pole, but I guess not. No worries. I'm glad you're such a thoughtful guy," she said, dishing out a bit of cat clawing sarcasm.

"Okay, Lucy, that's enough. This conversation is over. You go back to teaching your little kids how to take naps, and I'll go back to fighting fires and looking out for my brothers."

"What did you say?" She could feel the heat travel her entire body, settling onto her cheeks. *Did he really just say what she thought he said? What a Neanderthal!* "Sam, you're darn right this discussion is over. I'm not going to explain to you what I do as a teacher. You're obviously not in tune with what educators do, so I'll just leave it at that. Have a nice day. Oh, and, Sam? Tell your *brother*, happy anniversary!" *Click.*

She gathered her bags and purse and began the trek to her apartment. Her eyes clouded with tears, making it difficult to see, and she couldn't wipe the tears away since her hands were full. She felt the concerned stares of the people she met and by the time she reached her apartment door, she was sobbing uncontrollably. Everyone knew something wasn't quite right with Lucy Carmichael.

He held the phone out and stared at it. *What the heck just happened?* He took a shift for a buddy so he could take his wife out for their anniversary dinner. She'd never understand the camaraderie the firemen shared. He shook his head, and then he turned his truck around and headed back to his apartment. He looked over at Charlie, curled in a ball, totally content and looking up at him with big brown eyes. "Guess we're not going to Denver." Sam shrugged then looked in his rearview mirror and punched the accelerator.

He wasn't planning on sitting around in his apartment, especially not after his disheartening phone call with Lucy. It bugged him to no end how she'd behaved. Maybe she was having a bad day? It wasn't like him to run from a fight, but with Lucy it was such raw emotion driving his decision to avoid any more harsh words. He really could see himself with her long term, falling for her hard, but if she was going to make him choose between his job and her, well she had another think coming.

"Okay, explain to me exactly what he said," Beth said, licking the salt from the rim of her margarita.

"He said he was only staying for the night, that he had a change of plans. And when I pressed him more about it, he copped an attitude and said I didn't know anything about his job. Then he took a low blow and said all I do is teach kids how to take naps." She moved her mouth to the straw and slurped her frozen strawberry margarita.

Beth strummed the table with her fingers. "What do you think he meant by not knowing about his job? He's a fireman. He puts out fires, duh." She licked more salt off the rim.

"Maybe the risk involved? I really don't know, and quite frankly, I don't care."

Beth shook her finger at her. "Tsk-tsk. Don't say that. You do too care." She smiled a wide grin.

Dropping her shoulders slightly, Lucy sighed. "I did care. But I don't know, Beth. He seemed odd on the phone. Distant like we hadn't spent any time together. I can't explain it. It's probably for the best that he didn't come."

"Let's order dinner," Beth said, picking up the menu.

"I wish I could say I'm hungry, but I've lost my appetite," Lucy said, slumping deeper into the booth.

Just then, the waiter stepped up to their table, ready to take their orders. Beth peered over the top of the menu to her friend and then returned to the menu. "We'll have the appetizer platter and two more drinks." She closed it and handed the menu to the waiter.

"Thanks, Beth."

"For what?" She wrinkled her forehead.

"For being my friend. I can't talk to my mom about this. She'd never understand. She thought it was strange to fall for him in the first place."

"Please. She only said that because she still has Josh on the brain." Beth smirked.

"True. Maybe I should look at him again as a possibility?"

Beth straightened her shoulders and then slapped the table hard, startling Lucy. Lucy widened her eyes when she saw the terrified look in her friend's eyes.

"Don't you dare do that. Not because your mom wants it. If you want it, then okay, but do not, under any circumstance, date Josh because she wants you to."

Lucy shook her head like she was shaking some cobwebs away. "Okay, I was just saying that because—"

"Because you're feeling sorry for yourself. What happened to the new and improved Lucy Carmichael?"

"She's gone, just like most of my heart."

"Okay, that's it. Let's change the subject before I jump in my car and go crazy on him."

Lucy examined one of the egg rolls from the platter the waiter had just placed down on their table, and then took a bite. "Good," she mumbled.

"I didn't want to bring it up yet, but I might as well tell you." Beth locked gazes with Lucy. "I got a teaching job in Idaho." A faint smile crossed her lips.

"That's great news," Lucy said, reaching for her hand.

"I leave in two weeks."

"Two weeks! Wow."

"But I want you to promise me that you'll come visit."

"Of course, Beth." She fought to keep her voice steady and emotion free.

The rest of the evening they talked about Idaho, teaching, and how delicious the appetizer platter tasted. Despite losing her appetite, Lucy managed to wolf down a couple of egg rolls and boneless chicken wings. Oh, and another frozen strawberry margarita.

SHE WISHED of all nights she had a furry little buddy curled up by her side, to make her feel better about the awful phone fight she'd had with Sam. Instead, she was forced to find solace in some sappy television show. She also wished Beth had extended their evening by stopping by to have a glass of wine with her. She didn't like to drink alone, but she understood why Beth couldn't. She only had two weeks to prepare for her move to Idaho.

Here it was, a Friday night, and instead of Sam getting all of her attention, she was clicking through television channels, finally settling on an oldie but goodie Hallmark movie. But when it started resembling her own situation, it gave her great pause. She wasn't about to let him go without a fight. Maybe he didn't know it, but Sam was about to find out just how important he was to her, and more importantly, what she'd do to make him understand.

Leaning back on her sofa, she absently gazed out the open window. She could see the trees bending softly in the breeze, the stars starting to light up the darkening night sky, and a few couples holding hands as they walked to their cars. She reclined on the couch, just to rest her eyes for a bit. It had been an emotional roller coaster with Sam breaking up with her, or was it she who broke up with him? She shook her head. And now with Beth soon leaving, it was too much to handle for a person who tried to control everything and make it perfect.

She dozed off falling into a dream state where she was back at the rodeo with Sam. He'd just sneaked a kiss for the fiftieth time, making her giggle, and she reached up and touched her face where Sam's lips had just brushed. Then her eyes popped open and she realized it was just a dream. Blowing out a deep breath, she sat up. *This is ridiculous.* She reached for her phone.

"You've reached Sam. I'm out fighting fires or something. Leave a message at the beep."

"Sam! Sam, this is Lucy. Please call me." She hung up and slammed her back against the sofa. "Sam, please, please call me."

CHAPTER 11

Pulling the stool closer to the rig's giant tires, Sam sprayed the tire cleaner and began to wipe. The radio in the background gave him some good loud music to drown his blues and the energy to polish the tires. But even the music couldn't mask heavy breathing. "Hey, Scotty, looks like you're getting a good workout." Sam eyed the sweat dripping from Scotty's forehead and arms.

Scotty held an arm weight in his hands and curled it, showing off his biceps. "Gotta stay pretty for the little lady," he said, grunting between lifts.

"Yeah, I wouldn't know about that." Sam turned back to the tire and continued to polish the rubber.

"What happened to Lucy?"

"She's history," Sam said rather bluntly. "Sorry, didn't mean to be so short with you, but we're through."

"After everything you said about her, she's history? I don't believe it. What happened?"

"She doesn't understand my job here. She's a teacher, so everything is fluff and roses."

"Huh. Well, I sure didn't get that impression of her when you told me about her. What changed? And why are you here today? I thought you were going to visit her?"

"I was, but when I told her I had to cut the trip short, she got a major attitude."

Scotty cocked his head. "That doesn't sound like sweet little Lucy. Are you sure you just didn't misunderstand her?"

Sam threw down the old white tee shirt he used as a rag and crossed his hands in his lap.

"I mean, I do have twenty-five years of experience. Women are a tricky bunch. They say one thing, but mean another. You have to read between the lines." He lowered his chin and peered down at Sam.

"Maybe, but when she went off the deep end, I just figured what's the use?"

"What's the use? Okay, Sam, this is the girl you couldn't stop talking about. I'd say that's the use. You better call her back and make things right. If you don't, it'll always haunt you." Scotty turned his back and started to move away.

"I don't have time now. It's after three. I'd get in super late there and then have to turn around and come back tomorrow."

"Hey, Pete," Scotty called out to one of the men who was about to lift a one-hundred-pound barbell.

Pete finished the lift then set it into the barbell rack. He rose slowly, wiping the sweat off his brow with a nearby towel. "Yeah?"

"Can you take the overtime shift that Sam was going to cover for me so I can take the wifey out to dinner? It's our twenty-fifth anniversary, and sort of a big thing." He shrugged.

Pete nodded. "Sure, I can do that."

Sam stood and put out his hand to Pete. "Thanks, man. I owe you."

"No worries, brother. You'd do it for me, right?"

Sam nodded. "In a minute."

Scotty and Sam watched as Pete made his way back over to the weight lifting area the crew had set up in a corner of the oversized garage.

"Thanks, Scotty." Sam slipped his arm around his shoulders and patted him.

"If you don't remember anything else I tell you,

remember this. The women in our lives—we have to keep them happy." He winked again and then laughed.

SAM DROVE BACK to his apartment and picked up his bag. It still sat on the living room floor. He made a quick call to Wanda and asked if she'd dog sit Charlie. He didn't have the heart to rustle him up from his favorite activity, sleeping. He patted him on the head, tossed him a doggy biscuit to find when he awoke, and then headed out the door.

He had six hours to come up with the best *I'm sorry* line in the entire world, and practiced out loud while he drove.

"I'm sorry for getting cross with you, Lucy." He shook his head.

"I'm sorry for being such a jerk to you on the phone. Can you forgive me?" He groaned. *That's lame.*

"I know. I'll sweep her off her feet, give her a big juicy kiss, and not say anything." He reached over and turned the radio up. It was getting late and he needed to stay alert for the drive ahead.

He followed the directions he'd punched into his navigation system in the truck, and in about five hours, due to record-breaking speeds, he drove into the apartment complex where she lived. He parked his truck and then called from his cell phone.

"Hello."

"Hey, Lucy, it's me."

"Hey, Sam," she said in a remorseful whisper.

"I got your message. I thought I'd return it by coming—"

She quickly cut him off. "Sam, let's just put those cross words behind us. I care about you. I want to be your partner and that means understanding everything you do, including your job. I want to share my life with you, and these stupid arguments are a result of the miles between us and nothing more. I'm sorry for being a needy girlfriend. Will you forgive me?"

With the phone to his ear, Sam made his way toward her apartment. He knocked once, still holding the phone to his ear. He could hear her gasp from the other side of the door after she'd peered into the door peephole. He wiped the sheepish grin off his face as he waited for her.

Opening the door, she greeted him with a warm smile. "What are you doing here?"

"May I come in?" he asked, not really answering her question.

She opened the door wider and stepped aside.

"Listen, I know I was a jerk to you on the phone," he

said, just like he'd practiced, but still not liking the way it sounded. "I'm sorry."

He was like a strong magnet, and she found herself stepping closer and closer toward him until she was right in front of him. He opened his arms wide and she stepped into them, resting her head on his chest.

He ran his hand up and down her back trying to get back into her good graces. Swallowing hard, he spoke softly. "I'm not used to having to explain everything to someone else. I've been alone for a long time, Lucy." He pulled back and looked deeply into her eyes, feeling his heart melt and yearn for her even more.

"My buddy, Scotty, asked me to work his shift so he could take his wife out to dinner … for their anniversary. I can always use the extra overtime money, so I said yes before thinking through about our plans. I'm truly sorry that I didn't place you first before Scotty. But I'm the only single guy on the crew, and our lives are already pretty crazy, so when one of my guys wants to take his wife out for dinner, I want to help him."

Lifting up on her tiptoes, she kissed him. "That's what I love about you, Sam. You really do care about others."

"And what I said about your teaching job—that was just plain uncalled for. I don't know why I said that." He shook his head in abhorrence over his behavior.

"I should have known you didn't really mean it.

That's what people do when they fight. They say and do things they'd never really say or do if they weren't arguing."

He pulled her closer. "Thanks for understanding. The good news is that Pete took the overtime shift, so I can stay for a couple of days. I got Wanda to watch Charlie …"

She wrapped her arms around his neck, pulling him down to meet her mouth. She ran her tongue between his lips, eliciting a groan. Lifting her up in his arms, he opened one eye and made a quick assessment the bedroom must be down the hall, and headed that way. Good graces indeed!

"GOOD MORNING." She held her arms open.

"Good morning. Something smells delicious." He eyed the stack of pancakes and bacon as he entered the kitchen.

"I don't know about you, but I'm ravenous." A coy smile appeared on her lips.

He drew in a deep breath and let it out as he pulled out a chair and sat.

"About today, what would you like to do?" She chewed on a piece of bacon, batting her eyelashes at him.

Winking, he craned his neck toward the bedroom. "I can think of a few things."

Her eyes never wavered from his. She reached out and rested her palm on his arm. Thoughts of his strong broad shoulders, his soft touch, and the way he ran his hands through her hair made the hairs on the back of her neck prickle. "I mean outside of the apartment."

He cupped her hand with his, keeping it hostage. "Oh, that. Well, let's see. I'd like to meet your folks, see a little bit of downtown, go out to dinner, and then … come back to the apartment." He nodded toward the hall, his eyes burning with desire.

"I called my mom this morning. They'll be home later today, so we can drop in quickly to say hello, and then go downtown. There's a live concert going on at one of the parks. We could grab some picnic items, and enjoy the music." She smiled, trying to stay focused, otherwise, no one was leaving the apartment.

"Mom, Dad, this is Sam." Lucy motioned to Sam.

Sam held out his hand and shook Paul's hand. "Nice to meet you," he said, grinning.

"Lucy tells us you're a fireman. That's a dangerous

job." Marjorie led them to the family room. "Iced tea, lemonade?"

"Lemonade sounds good," Sam said, perking up.

"Lucy, why don't you come help me while Sam and your father get acquainted?"

She whispered in Sam's ear. "Travel with caution." She patted him on the shoulder then met her mom in the kitchen.

"Lucy is our only child. Do you have siblings?"

"Yes, my sister Wanda."

"Are your parents alive?"

Here comes the third degree she warned me about. "My dad is gone."

"I'm sorry to hear that."

"It was a long time ago," he said, trying to end that part of the interrogation.

"How long have you been a firefighter?"

"Oh, let's see. I'm starting my eighth year."

"I guess you'll be making a career of it, then?" Paul nodded.

"Yes, I love being a firefighter."

"Firemen are away from home a lot, though, right?" Paul's piercing eyes made Sam uncomfortable.

"True, we are. The station is like a home away from home. The guys I work with are like family." Sam tipped his chin a few times.

Paul scratched his chin. "I'm just trying to figure out how you two are going to make this relationship work. It's one thing about the distance, but then throw in your odd hours, and well, I see that as a recipe for disaster."

"Here we are, cold lemonade," Marjorie called out, carrying a tray with glasses.

Lucy snuggled next to Sam and laid her hand on his thigh. Touching him like that stirred deep feelings.

"Your dad was just asking me about our long-distance relationship." Sam tightened his lips as he gave Lucy a nod.

Lucy cut her eyes toward her dad. "Dad, this is between Sam and I how we handle our relationship." She handed Same a glass from the tray and then retrieved one for herself.

"I know, dear. I was just merely asking how it would work out, that's all." He slurped his drink, not making eye contact with her.

"I think we'll work it out. I really care about your daughter."

"I guess we're a bit over protective," Marjorie said.

"I understand your desire to protect your only child. I only ask you give me a chance," Sam turned to Lucy and smiled.

"Mom." Lucy stood. "Either we need to change the subject or we're leaving."

"Lucy, I'm sorry for giving Sam the third degree. I didn't do it intentionally. We love you and are just worried about how a long distance relationship is going to work. But you're a grown woman, can make your own decisions. We like Sam and look forward to getting to know him better." Paul dropped his head slightly then slowly raised his eyes to meet Lucy's. "You'll always be our little girl. I guess I overreacted."

"We both overreacted," Marjorie said stepping close to Paul and lacing her arm in his.

She dropped Sam's hand and sighed. Turning around she faced her father. "Dad, you know I love you and I respect you. I guess I got a little hot under the collar with the third degree, but most importantly, I hate it when Mom behaves like some little schoolgirl trying to make nice with everyone. It just irks me to no end. And the real problem is, I'm beginning to behave like that with Sam, and I don't want to!"

"Honey," Paul said, stepping forward. "Mom just wants everything to be perfect. When she sees the apple-cart upset, it drives her to behave this way. You know that about her. It's nothing new." His softness made her weak.

Lucy looked beyond her dad. Sam stood off to her side, with his head bowed. Her mother stood about ten feet back, twisting her hands, clearly upset. She walked around her dad and stood facing her mom. "I'm sorry, Mom. I shouldn't have flown off the handle like that. It just drives me crazy when you try to sugarcoat everything. But I know … it's just your way." Lucy reached for her hands.

Marjorie laced her fingers with her daughter's. "I'm trying to stop doing that, but it's hard. You know for so many years—"

Lucy pulled her finger to her mouth to silence her mom. "It's okay. We're all frail; we all have insecurities and faults. We're human. I love you, and I'm sorry."

Her dad came up behind them and wrapped his arms around his family. "We love you, Lucy." He kissed the top of her head.

"Love you, too."

Sam quickly brushed the tear that rolled down his cheek. He hadn't been moved this much in a long time. Lucy and her little dysfunctional family made him feel at ease, less embarrassed about his own family.

"You guys go out and enjoy the sunshine and downtown. If we don't see you again before you head back to Dodge City, be safe. It was so nice meeting you." Paul walked them to the door with Marjorie by his side.

"Would you two like some lemonade or chocolate chip cookies for the road?" Marjorie asked.

Lucy dropped her shoulders. It was no use. Marjorie

would always mother her to death. She looked over at Sam.

Shrugging, he said, "Cookies sound good."

THEY STOPPED at one of the local grocery stores and purchased some cheese, salami, crackers, a bottle of wine, and some plastic glasses. Sam said he had a corkscrew in the truck, and she already knew he had a blanket. They drove out to the park where the music festival was going on, and found a shady spot under a huge oak tree.

"Before we say or do anything else, let me just say that I really like your parents. Even with the third degree from Paul. I really respect that he only wants the best for you."

"Really? You got all of that from a twenty-minute visit?" She smirked.

"I did. And let's talk about Marjorie. First of all, she makes killer lemonade and chocolate chip cookies." He held up a giant cookie and took a bite.

Lucy laughed. "Help me with the wine." She handed him the bottle.

"She's a little too sensitive, and it could be that is where you got some of your sensitivity from, but it's all good." He peeled the foil from around the bottle, exposing the cork, and then plunged in the corkscrew, grunting as he twisted it up and out of the bottle neck.

"Too sensitive? You think I'm too sensitive?" She squared her shoulders and looked out into the grassy area where several couples sat close together while their children laughed and ran around, burning off energy with the occasional dog running after them and barking.

"Just a tad, but I think it's cute." He poured her a glass and offered it to her.

She took it and then resumed her people watching.

"Lucy Carmichael, you know I care about you. Even with all your insecurities and OCD. If you are willing to take me on with my messy apartment, tongue wagging dog who drools, and my gossipy sister, then we're a match made in heaven." He lifted his glass, waiting for her to toast.

She slowly raised her glass to meet his.

"I'm not great with toasts, but here's a stab at one." He drew in his bottom lip and studied her fast. "I know we've got something special, and I'm willing to work through all obstacles to make it work. Even the distance, if that's the way it has to be." He clanked her glass.

"I'm willing to do whatever it takes to make this work, even if it means tossing your keys into the pond." Her eyes drifted to the water feature in the distance. "And locking you inside my apartment so I can have you morning, noon, and night." She gave him a sheepish grin then clanked his glass, finally drawing in a taste of the Chardonnay.

He moved in closer. She could feel the warmth of his breath as he inched his way closer toward her mouth. "See? You're one sexy thing." He pressed his mouth to hers, enjoying the sweet taste of the wine.

SHE WRAPPED her arms around his waist and they slowly made their way to his parked truck. It'd been the best couple of days of her life. And now it was ending. "I don't want you to leave."

"I don't want to leave, but I have to. When can you come visit me?" He set his bag down on the ground, and then backed up against his truck, pulling her in. He wrapped his arms around her waist and pulled her deeper between his legs.

"School starts in three weeks. I can probably visit during the holidays." She could feel him as she pressed against him, and it made it all that more difficult to let him leave.

"Man, I don't know if I can wait that long." His eyes peered at her through half closed lids.

A tear rolled down her cheek then another. Soon the waterworks came on full force.

"Oh, baby, I didn't mean to upset you." He gently wiped them away with his fingers.

She drew in his woodsy scent as he touched her and it just made the tears flow more. "You better leave before I won't let you," she said, choking back tears.

"Okay, I'll call you while I'm on the road as long as I have coverage. Don't worry about me, don't think the worst, and lastly, don't think anything bad about us. I love you, I want you, and if anything changes, I'll let you know." He dropped a kiss on her forehead.

She stared blankly at him.

"What? Okay, did I say something wrong? I'm not leaving here until we get it straight." He studied her face hard.

She moistened her lips. "You said you love me." She swallowed down the lump that formed in her throat. "You love me?" Her voice climbed a little higher.

"Yes, silly. I love you." He circled his fingers in her belt loops and pulled her in. "Don't you love me, too?" He rocked her back and forth.

"Yes, but I was afraid to say it."

"Okay, Marjorie." He wrinkled his forehead.

She play slapped his arm. "Don't call me that." She laughed.

"Well, what happened to saying what you mean?"

She tipped her forehead. "You're right. I have to start practicing what I preach."

"We'll get through it. You know why?" He lowered his chin and gazed at her eyes.

"Because we love each other?" she squeaked out as a question.

"That's right. And anything worth having, is well … not always easy, but in the end, it'll be what holds us together. Like glue." He winked.

"Okay, Sam, you better get on the road before I really handcuff you to my headboard." She stepped out of his reach and crossed her arms.

A low belly laugh escaped his lips as he jumped inside his truck and started the engine. Rolling down the window, he held out his hand, motioning her to take hold of it as the truck crept forward.

She reticently took it, giving him one last squeeze. "Bye, Sam. Love you. Call me," she said as she let go, watching him drive away.

"Hey," he shouted, looking back at her. "Just for the record—do you really have handcuffs?"

Before she could reply, he winked, flashed a wide grin, and accelerated away from her.

CHAPTER 12

This was harder than anything she'd ever experienced before. Well, almost, but this came darn close. She didn't like the achy feeling in her heart after she sobbed nonstop, causing her face to balloon, her lids to swell, and her tear ducts to become void of any more tears. It was just too much for her to handle. But what could she do?

She called it an early evening, and with the remote to the television, a bowl of buttered popcorn, a bag of peanut M&M's, and a sugary drink, she was all set to drown out her sorrows by watching what else? A love story. But after three romantic scenes that were three too many, she changed the channel to something less stirring and began to search the internet on her tablet.

One minute she was looking up recipes, the next hairstyles, and before she realized it, she was on the Dodge City home page. She stared at the listing, and after about two minutes of her finger hovering above the text, she pressed her finger to the link that read job openings.

She had to read the announcement several times before it sunk in. Could this really be a teaching position open? She settled into the comfy sofa, staring up at the television screen just in time to get distracted by a brother and sister team on a remodeling show gutting an entire bathroom. Her eyes strayed back down to her tablet. She read all the qualifications for the job and then hit the next link that took her to an online application. She began to type in the preliminary information, having to stop to retrieve some documents for dates, and then resumed filling out the application. When she finished, her finger hovered over the final button, submit. What if he doesn't want me there? What if I move there and it doesn't work out? What if …

Her phone began to vibrate on the glass top of the coffee table, jolting her back to reality. She quickly moved the tablet out of her reach and answered the phone.

"Hello, Sam! Where are you?"

"I just pulled in at my apartment complex. What are you doing?"

"I'm sitting here in my ugliest pajamas, eating

snacks … and watching a love story." She left out the part about the job. She hadn't hit the submit button yet, anyway.

He chuckled under his breath. "Oh-oh, that doesn't sound good."

"I miss you already."

"I miss you, too. What are we going to do about that? It's only been six hours."

"I could come to Dodge City."

"Come to Dodge City? You mean before the holidays?"

She pulled her legs up and sat cross-legged. She reached for the tablet and focused on the screen. "No, like maybe permanently?" She cringed at the thought of him laughing. She drew in her bottom lip and chewed it—her anxiety at an all-time high right then.

"That would be great, hon, but what about your job? Aren't you getting your classroom ready and all of that?"

"Well, I was sitting here watching lovers on the television screen and couldn't take much more of it, so I began to search the web on my tablet. I was honestly looking for new recipes. I mean, how many ways can you fix chicken? Anyway, then I realized my hair was getting a bit long and stringy and thought I'd check out hairstyles."

"I love your hair," he interjected loudly.

"I know, just a trim, but then … I found myself on the Dodge City home page."

"The home page?

"Uh-huh. I found job listings, too."

"And you found a teaching job here?" he said, ruining her big surprise.

"Yes! An elementary teacher position is open. Said it was an emergency hire and they need all applications in by midnight tomorrow." She uncrossed her legs and then stretched out on the sofa, staring at the ceiling. "Isn't that great? I can get the job, move there, and we can be together all the time."

"Okay, hold on, Lucy. You have to get the job first."

Twirling her locks, she pushed out her bottom lip and blinked a couple of times. *Maybe it did sound a bit foolish.* "I know, but I'm more than qualified. Don't you know anyone who could pull a few strings for me?"

He laughed in her ear. "I'll see what I can do. Have you already applied?"

"Not yet. I wanted to make sure you'd be alright with it," she said.

"Hit that submit button. I'll talk to you tomorrow. Oh, and, Lucy?"

She nodded, although she was aware he couldn't see her. "Yes?"

"I love you."

She closed her eyes and drew in a deep breath. "I love you, too."

"THANKS FOR COMING BY, BETH." Lucy walked Beth down to her car, trying to keep the tears away. She really appreciated her stopping by on her way to Idaho. "Drive safely," Lucy said, trying to stay strong, but somehow the words still crackled with sentiment.

Beth opened her car door and slid in.

Lucy bent down and peered into the back seat. She could see boxes and suitcases stacked to the roofline. "Can you see out the back?" She laughed.

"That's what these are for," Beth said, pointing to the side mirrors.

Lucy nodded.

"Well, I better get on the road. I'll call you."

Lucy stepped back and flipped a wave to Beth as she drove off. Turning around, she walked back to her apartment with her head hanging low, feeling the loss of her best friend.

IT'D BEEN a week since she'd hit the submit button, and

the only correspondence she'd received so far was a computer-generated email telling her they'd received her application. In one week, school would start. She might as well just forget about the job in Dodge City. It wasn't going to happen. It was too much of a long shot.

She went over to her folks' house for dinner. She wasn't really in the mood for conversation, or good food for that matter, but her parents didn't have anything to do with the way she was feeling.

"Aren't you hungry?" Marjorie asked, nodding toward her mostly untouched food.

Lucy pushed the spaghetti around her plate with her fork and sighed. "Not really."

"Everything alright with Sam?" Paul asked, trying to engage his daughter in conversation.

"Yeah," she replied, and then scooted the green beans around her plate before finally putting her fork down. "I better get home."

"You haven't even finished your dinner. I made strawberry shortcake for dessert, but—"

"Marjorie, she isn't a child. Just because she didn't finish her dinner doesn't mean she can't have dessert." He shook his head then resumed eating.

"I don't want any dessert. I just want to go home."

"Lucille Carmichael, I know something is up. Spill the beans right now." Her mother shot her a stern look.

She perked up when she heard this new wave of straightforward talk and her full name escaping her mother's lips. She couldn't remember the last time they'd called her Lucille.

"I'm lonely. I miss Sam, and I applied for this job in Dodge City, but haven't heard anything back," she rattled on.

Her dad put his fork down and sat straight up in the hardback chair. Her mother dropped hers, and it pinged across the china.

"You applied for a job there?" her dad asked.

"Yes. Yes, I did. But don't worry, I won't get it. School starts in exactly six days. There's no way I could get moved there and begin a new job in six days."

CHAPTER 13

Lucy and her mother stood back as Paul loaded the car. She laced her arm with her mother's feeling her tremble slightly. "It's okay, mom. This feels so right." The corners of her mouth curled up.

"I know dear. It just happened so quickly."

"I was very fortunate that Denver Elementary was so understanding about my quick departure."

"Good teachers are hard to find." Marjorie placed her hand on Lucy's arm and squeezed it.

"Okay, this is the last of it," Paul said, lifting a box and sliding it into the back of her car. He brushed his hands along his pants and stood back as she closed her trunk.

"I guess this is it, then." Lucy's eyes began to well up.

"After you get settled, we'll come for a visit," he said.

Lucy looked beyond her dad to see her mother sobbing in her hands. "Mom, I'm just a few hours away." She held her arms out, and Marjorie shuffled toward her, sliding into her arms. Lucy wrapped them around her and kissed her cheek. "I'm going to be with Sam, Mom," she whispered.

Marjorie tried to talk, but the words came out in bits, choked by her emotions. She brushed the tears aside and then gained her composure. "I know, and I'm happy for you."

"You better get on the road, young lady," Paul said, his voice cracking after seeing the two embrace.

Lucy let her mother out of her hold and then held out her arms to her dad. "You didn't think I was going to let you go without a bear hug, did you?" The little girl in her recalled his warm snuggly hugs. With his head lowered, he melted into her arms and squeezed her just like the old days. She ran her hands along the wispy and now grey hair that grew on his arms. "I love you, Dad."

"I love you, too, Lucy girl." He wiped the few tears that trailed down his cheeks and quickly regained his composure. "If you need anything …"

"I know, pick up the phone and call."

"That's right. And if Sam turns out to be a turd then you know the way back home."

When he gave her the look that said he really meant

it, she knew he really meant it. "I got it. No worries." She placed a hand on her car door.

"We love you, Lucy," her mom called out.

She opened the car door and slid in. She watched through the mirror as her parents stood by, wiping their tears and trying to be cheerful. It must be pretty hard to watch your only child move away. She hit the button and released the window. Sticking her hand out, Lucy waved goodbye. "Love you, guys. Wish me luck."

"You got this," Paul yelled.

"Okay, let's see. Please put the couch over by the window."

The two movers started to move as she'd directed.

"No wait. Not by the window, over here," she said, motioning toward the opposite wall of the window.

The two movers started to head toward the wall.

"Wait."

The movers grunted then put the couch down. "Miss, make up your mind."

She thumped her finger to her chin and studied the room. "Okay, over there," she said, pointing to the last location she'd asked them to put it.

The poor movers had had it with her. She changed her

mind on furniture placement with just about every item. The OCD came out in full force.

THERE WASN'T much time for dallying because she had a classroom still to decorate. Class started the following day, and Lucy, not used to being behind on stuff, found this to aggravate her already elevated OCD.

Sam helped by setting up the hamster cage and picking out a furry little baby. He also went down to the supply room and brought in rolls of paper, bottles of paint, and other art supplies. On each desk, Lucy placed a package of colored pencils as her classroom warming gift to each student. This would be a great school year.

They stood back and admired their speedy decorating job. Sam slid his arm around her waist and pulled her close. "I think we make a great decorating duo, don't you?" His eyes floated from the desks to the little hamster who decided to try out his wheel, to Lucy's desk that had her calendar and pencil holder in the shape of a shiny red apple.

"I think we did a great job. I can't believe I'm here." She snuggled closer.

"I can't either, but I'm really happy it worked out. They say where there is a will …" He kissed her cheek.

"Sam?"

"Yes, babe?"

"If I ever get to be a burden to you, or you just don't want to be with me anymore, don't beat around the bush telling me, okay?"

"Now, Lucy … why are you saying that? You just moved here."

"I guess I think everything is just too perfect. I'm waiting for the other shoe to drop."

"Why can't good things happen for us? I mean, we're good people. We have community driven professions, we love people, we are doing good things for our city. Why can't we be madly in love and everything be perfect?" His eyes held hers.

"True. I'm just so happy to be yours." She blinked, then, letting him know she wanted a kiss, raised her chin so he could have full access to her hungry lips.

He took the hint, pulling her in and kissing her deeply.

Realizing their chemistry was over the moon hot, Lucy shook off the warm all over feeling his kisses gave her. "Well, I think I'm ready for tomorrow. Let's go get some dinner." She slid her purse over her shoulder and moved toward the light switch.

Standing in the hall, they took one last look at the

classroom. Lucy reached up and turned the light off then pulled the door closed.

"So are you all settled into your apartment?" Wanda pulled a slice of pizza from the silver round pan and placed it on her plate. She shook some red pepper flakes and cheese on it before trying a bite.

"Yes, I am. I probably have a few things to tweak, but overall, yes, I'm settled. I'll have you over soon." Lucy pulled a slice of pizza from the pan.

"Do you like the apartment complex?" Wanda poured beer in her glass from the pitcher then poured the others.

"I do. In fact, I met one of my neighbors already. Not sure which apartment she lives in, though. We met at the garbage collection area. She said she is a dispatcher for a trucking company. I think she said her name was Arletta."

Sam knocked shoulders with Lucy. "Hey, don't go making friends just yet. I don't want to give up my time to anybody else." He winked, making her blush.

"You'll always be my number one friend." She nuzzled his nose with hers.

"Okay, you guys, get a room or something," Wanda said, bringing her beer glass to her lips.

Lucy's cheeks filled with color. "Sorry," she squeaked out.

"Just kidding. Glad you guys are *so* much in love."

Sam glanced at his watch. "As much as I have enjoyed this, I must call it an evening. I have a long shift coming up." He grabbed another slice and wolfed it down.

"I have an early day, too. My first day on the job," Lucy said, beaming ear to ear.

"I have the day off tomorrow, so I'm going to sleep in, then drive out to the lake. We only have a few more weeks of this warm weather. I'm going to take advantage of it." Wanda smiled.

Sam and Lucy waved to Wanda as she drove off then he drove Lucy home.

"I'd ask you to come up, but I know you need your rest," she said, trying to contain her desire to be alone with him.

"Rain check, okay?" He beckoned her to join him in a kiss.

He didn't have to wait too long. Her lips met his, setting off a low groan from him.

"Well, maybe I'll come up for just a few minutes." A suggestive grin crossed his face, making her heart thump inside her chest.

CHAPTER 14

"Good morning, class. My name is Ms. Carmichael. I'm so happy to have each of you in my class. I've left a little something on each of your desks. It's a welcome gift from me to you. I hope our school year is filled with fun, challenges, and lots of learning. As part of our orientation today, I'd like for you to get up and walk around the classroom and get comfortable with your new surroundings. We have a classroom mascot over there," she said, motioning to the large clear cage with lots of colorful tunnels for the critter to travel through, "that needs a name, and don't forget to check out the arts and crafts center."

The children rose from their desks quietly and made their way around the classroom. She watched as they interacted and introduced themselves to one another. It was all part of her plan. She found that many children were insecure, and when you asked them to stand and introduce themselves it just added to their insecurity. This way, the children were interacting and mingling, not even realizing they were socializing. It worked every time. She crossed her arms and smiled.

When the bell rang, signaling the day had come to an end, Lucy was pretty exhausted. It had been a very hectic week moving, getting settled into her apartment, decorating the classroom, and preparing for her first day. All she wanted to do was put her feet up, have a glass of wine, and not think about too much of anything. Of course, she couldn't wait to hear Sam's voice and tell him all about her day.

In the middle of their talk, the alarm sounded. He'd already informed her that if that ever happened while they were talking, he'd have to hang up, and quickly. She got in a quick I love you before he disconnected the call. She shuffled into the kitchen and opened the refrigerator door and peered in. She grabbed the carton of eggs.

Cracking two eggs into a bowl, she began to whip them around. She added salt and pepper, and then stirred them into her hot pan. As they cooked, she moved the eggs around with the spatula, and when they were cooked the way she liked them, she scooped them out of the pan and onto her plate, adding a little shredded cheese. She poured herself a glass of red wine and took her dinner to the living room.

She forked some hot eggs with melted cheese and brought it to her mouth, blowing on it just a tad before tasting it. She went for her second bite but didn't quite make it. Someone was knocking at her door.

She peered through the peephole, and spied on her new neighbor standing outside. She opened the door with a smile.

"Hey, neighbor. Lucy, right?" Arletta rocked back on her heels and flashed a wide grin.

"Yes, and you're Arletta, right?"

"Yes! Most people can't remember my name. It's so *unique* they say." She chuckled.

"I was just having dinner. Can I offer you a glass of wine?" Lucy opened the door wider.

"Oh, that sounds great." Arletta entered the apartment and without waiting, made her way toward the empty chair and sat.

Lucy went to the kitchen and poured Arletta her wine. "Here you go," she said, offering her the glass.

"Please, finish your dinner. I'll just sip mine," she said, motioning toward Lucy's plate.

"Oh, you haven't had dinner? I'm sorry for not asking. I can quickly whip you up some scrambled eggs." Lucy pushed her eggs around on the plate.

"No, this will be just fine. It's been a long day. I've had to re-route drivers because of bad weather all darn day, and not to mention, a missing truck full of someone's household." She looked around Lucy's apartment. "I see that you got your stuff okay."

"Yes, everything arrived and in one piece." She pushed her plate away. She didn't feel like eating in front of Arletta.

"So, you said you're a teacher over at the elementary school?" She drew in a sip of her wine.

"Yes, today was my first day. The children were so receptive to me."

"That's good because children can be so fickle, like men." She twisted her mouth tightly and tipped her head.

Lucy crossed her legs. "Well, I've always had a special way with children. I guess you could say it was my calling to become a teacher." She shrugged her shoulders a few times.

"I guess you have a way with handsome firemen, too." Arletta winked.

Now Lucy didn't like the way that rolled off of Arletta's lips. She pursed her lips tightly before answering her. Just like she told the children in her classroom, she wanted to choose her words carefully, because words can hurt, too. "I'm not sure I understand what you mean?"

That should give her the benefit of the doubt. Lucy peered at her through half closed lids.

"Oh, I didn't mean anything by it. It's sort of quick, though. You just moved in and are already entertaining handsome men."

Lucy crossed her arms. "First of all, I've known Sam for a while. True, I just moved here, but … wait a second. Why am I explaining all this to you?"

"Oh, that's cool. I can't seem to make any relationship last longer than a couple of months. Either they're momma's boys, or drawn back into the arms of their former wives or girlfriends, or they have money issues. If it isn't one thing then it's another."

Lucy sighed. Arletta was something else. "Well, it just sounds like you've had a few bad apples. I didn't have the best of luck in men, either. Then I met Sam."

"I don't know if I could date a fireman. They're always gone or always in danger."

"Arletta, these are the sacrifices one makes when it's true love." She found her conversation with her more exhausting than running a classroom filled with eight-year olds.

"Well, I guess I better get back to my four walls." Arletta stood.

"Thanks for stopping by. Maybe we can have lunch some day?" Lucy walked her to the door.

"Maybe, but seems like I'm always working, and when I'm not, I'm over at my mom's helping her."

"Oh, is she ill?" Lucy asked.

"She's on lots of medication for rheumatoid arthritis, depression, and diabetes."

"Wow. That's quite a bit of stuff she's dealing with."

"She's dealing with? I'm the one who has to spend all my free time helping her because she won't ask anyone else. No wonder I can't keep a boyfriend. I wouldn't even want to date me." She snorted then opened the door to let herself out. "Thanks again for the wine."

Lucy tapped Arletta on the shoulder.

She turned around with slouched shoulders. "I know, I must sound like a negative Nellie."

"I didn't always have it easy either, Arletta. And there was a time or two when I sounded like the sky was always falling, but then I realized that so many are worse off than me. I know it doesn't seem like it when you're stuck right dab in the middle of it, but, if you let someone in to help you sort it all out, then maybe you'll have a different perspective. Open your heart and mind to all kinds of possibilities." She squeezed Arletta's shoulder then let her hand fall away.

Arletta pulled in her bottom lip. "I know, but it's so hard. I mean, I'm twenty-eight years old, work for a trucking company by day, and a nursemaid by night and weekends. I have no life."

"It's your mother, though. Maybe if we find some relief for you, you'd see that she's not really a burden. I know you must love her."

"We don't have funds for that. That's another issue. We're flat broke. The only asset she has is her home."

"Okay, Arletta, let me sleep on this. I'm new to town, but I know there has to be organizations here that can help. Will you allow me to check?" She peered at her through half closed lids.

"Sure, but I've been through them all. They only help those who have big bucks. They couldn't care less about us."

"Have a good evening, Arletta. I'll be in touch." Lucy closed the door and rested her back against it. This new friend of hers was a challenge, but nothing quite thrilled Lucy as much as a good challenge.

"OKAY, your new friend Arletta is exhausting, Lucy!" Beth bellowed into the phone. "Do you really want to deal with all of that?"

Lucy took in a deep breath and let it out slowly. "Yes. Yes, I do. And you know why?"

"No, but I think you're about to tell me." Beth giggled.

"Under the deep cover of anger and cynicism is a free spirit just trying to cope with the hand she's been given."

"She sounds like a wackadoodle and you should take Sam's advice and not get involved."

"He didn't say not to get involved. He said to tread lightly. There's a difference."

"Well, whatever. Anyway, let's talk about our men, shall we?"

The two women shared stories about their love lives and new teaching jobs. It seemed they both were doing well and were happy as clams. As much as she missed Beth and they vowed to be friends forever, Lucy also knew that with all the miles between them, they'd have to accept that their friendship would now consist of chats via the telephone mostly, although they did try to keep the dream alive by talking about visiting. Who knows, maybe it would materialize.

SAM STRETCHED out on his sofa and fell asleep with Charlie at his feet. It had been another exhausting week fighting one fire after another. He never wished for winter to arrive so much. A good soaking and all the fire threat would be gone. He longed to wrap Lucy up in his arms and nibble on her, make her tingle all over, and then succumb to his every wish, but the truth of the matter was, he'd probably fall asleep in the middle of something, and that wouldn't bode well for him.

A light rap on his door woke Charlie up, causing him to protest with a few mild barks. Sam rubbed his eyes and yawned, squinting to see the time somewhere. He picked up his cell phone. It was seven o'clock. He rose from the couch, tripping over his shoes. He grabbed the doorknob and opened the door. "Hey, babe. What's up?" He covered his mouth to hide his yawn.

"I'm sorry to just barge in on you, but I need your help."

He shook his head then stumbled over to the couch and plopped down, patting the seat next to him.

She picked up a crumpled shirt and pressed it open with her hands and then eased it over the back of the couch before she sat down.

He looped his arm over her shoulders. "What's the deal?"

"I haven't seen you in days. I miss you." She snuggled deeper under his arm.

"I know, it's been brutal. I'm praying for rain." He crossed his feet at the ankles and rubbed his socked feet together.

"I miss your touch, your kisses." She turned toward him so he could have easy access to her mouth. He didn't move an inch. She moistened her dry mouth. "Kisses …" she repeated, puckering up.

Running his hand through his tousled locks, he laughed. "Sorry. Still waking up. I'm not usually this dense when it comes to what women want."

"Are you off this weekend?" She cupped his face, enjoying the feel of his five o'clock shadow. She trailed kisses from his lips to his cheek and back to his lips. "I'm really lonely," she said, with a throaty laugh and a pouty look before kissing him deeper, letting him know just how lonely.

He kissed her back but it wasn't with the same intensity she'd come to love and appreciate.

She took notice. "I shouldn't have come over without calling. I'm sorry." She stood, brushing down any wrinkles that may have appeared. She flipped her hair back with one hand and then tucked some strands behind her ear. "I'm normally not this needy." She lowered her gaze.

He grunted as he stood. "You're not needy. But even if you were, I think it's cute. It's just that I'm beat, Lucy. I couldn't perform—"

Her fingers rested on his lips and stopped him from speaking. "No apologies. I get it. You're tired, and rightfully so." She released her finger from his mouth and dropped a quick kiss on his lips.

He wrapped his arms around her waist and pulled her in. "But I do love you and I'm glad you stopped over." He gave her a quick peck. Charlie barked, getting their attention.

"Oh, Charlie," Lucy said, bending over and rubbing his back.

"I'll be ready for the weekend, I promise."

She tilted her head and narrowed her eyes. At the same time they both said, "Unless an emergency comes up." She shook her head. "I'm beginning to understand just how much of an adjustment being involved with a fireman really is."

He held her hand as he walked her out. "I'll call you soon."

Sam plopped back down on the sofa after she left, hoping with all of his might that he could hang on to her. It would take a really understanding woman to be satisfied with broken dates, sleepless nights, and everything else that came attached to this profession. He didn't know if over time she'd adjust, but he hoped so. He loved her that much, but right now he loved sleep more. *The life of a fireman, sigh.* He closed his eyes and nodded off. Charlie resumed his sleeping position at the foot of the couch and soon both boys were snoring softly.

CHAPTER 15

One thing was for certain, Lucy always kept her word. When she had a free moment, she checked out some organizations that specialized in caring for the elderly and the sick. She didn't have any problem finding a few promising leads.

She didn't make any appointments with any of the agencies, only taking down all their information so Arletta could make an informed decision. Lucy had neglected to ask what apartment she lived in so she made a quick stop in the complex manager's office. It was like pulling teeth to get the information from the assistant manager. She had to practically promise to name her first-born after her to get Arletta's apartment number.

Lucy made her way to the stairs. Arletta apparently

lived on the second floor. As she approached the door, she could hear loud music coming from her apartment. She rapped on the door a couple of times before she answered.

"Whoa, hey." Arletta turned her back and left Lucy standing there.

She finally stepped in when she figured out this was how she greeted folks to enter her dwelling. "Listen, I have some news about certain agencies that can help you and your mother." She looked around the dimly lit room and stretched her gaze around as far as she could see. It was pretty tidy, just dark and depressing.

"Have a seat." Arletta turned the music way down so they could talk. "What did you find out?" She plopped down on an upholstered hassock and laced her fingers together.

Lucy produced the small notepad from her pocket. "Well, let's see. There is this group called Visiting Angels. They'll come and sit with your mom, help with chores, and even help her with showers. Then, ah, let's see, oh, yes, another group that is part of the Catholic Church here in town offered similar help and you don't have to be Catholic to partake in their services." Lucy scanned her notes. "Oh, and I also discovered another agency similar to Visiting Angels … what was their name …"

Clearing her throat loud and clear, Arletta held up a hand. "Stop. Don't read any more stuff to me."

Lucy looked up from her notes. "Why? I thought you'd be pleased about the level of services available. It's a win-win for you both. You can get some respite care, and your mom can get some care from other professionals." She tried to make sense of Arletta's hesitation but to no avail.

"I told you before … no funds. The bank is broke. We don't have any money to pay these people."

"Well, if you let me finish, I also found out something regarding a reverse mortgage. Have you heard about that?" Lucy crossed her arms and her legs.

"I think so."

"You mentioned your mom owns her house. The bank will give her so much money based on the equity in the home. She doesn't have to make payments, and you as the heir don't have to square up with the bank until after she's gone. It's a perfect solution, don't you think?" Lucy held her breath as she waited for doubting Arletta to respond.

"I guess. I never checked into that before. I've seen the commercials about it, though." Arletta's eyes sparkled for the first time since Lucy had met her.

"Okay, then here's the name of the bank in town that is offering these types of mortgages, and the loan officer's name and number. Call them as soon as you can. These agencies told me they schedule visits a month in advance, but they are quite sure they can squeeze a few in for your mom." Lucy stood.

Arletta remained sitting for a few seconds then bolted straight up and wrapped her arms around Lucy, squeezing her tightly. "Thank you for helping me. I feel like a load has been lifted from my shoulders."

Lucy giggled as she stepped back from her hold. This was a different side of her. "Arletta, never take on such a load that it makes you sad and lonely. I've done that before. It's not healthy or wise. Help is always available, you just have to ask." Lucy smiled at her new friend as she crossed over to the front door. "Please let me know if you need any help with anything. I'm glad to help."

"I just might do that."

"How's your friend Arletta doing?" Beth asked, during one of their phone calls.

"Okay, remember how everything was awful and it was always poor, pitiful me with her? Well, now it's everything is just fine and dandy, life couldn't be any better, and if I have to hear one more time how thankful she is that I intervened, I'm going to scream," Lucy growled into the phone.

"Let me get this straight. You, Ms. the world is your oyster, are upset with Arletta because she's turned a new leaf? You should be ashamed of yourself."

"I know, and I am. It's just that she's so positive now. I kind of miss the old Arletta."

"Well, maybe some of the old Arletta will come back after she settles in with this new system of help and money," Beth said, trying to convince Lucy that all would be well.

"I guess I should be careful what I wish for. I just have to get used to it."

"How's that handsome fireman doing?"

Thankful they had changed the subject, Lucy smiled at the thought of him and his sexy dimples. "He's good," she said, purring like a kitten.

"Ha ha," her friend said, totally getting her drift.

"How about Caleb. How's he treating you?"

"Oh, let's just say we can't get enough of each other."

"And your new school?" Lucy was curious how Beth found her new surroundings, because she really loved the Dodge City school district.

"They are outstanding. I haven't had a single parent complaint."

Lucy laughed so hard her sides hurt. "Yeah, you troublemaker," she quipped.

"It was nice to hear from you. Glad all is well. Talk soon, huh?" Beth said.

Lucy marched into the kitchen and then did a little dance in front of the sink. Helping Arletta and reaching out to Beth, her day seemed complete. Now all she needed was some alone time with Sam. She glanced at the clock on the stove and did a quick calculation. Sixteen more hours and she'd be in the arms of the man she loved!

She cleaned her apartment, which took her all of ten minutes. This was the advantage to having OCD. Hardly ever was anything out of place—ever. She gathered the little garbage collected and made a quick stop out to the collection gathering site where all the big green containers were. She'd just lifted the lid and dumped the bag in, when she heard Arletta's voice.

"Good day, neighbor," she sang out.

A slow grin moved across Lucy's mouth as she twirled around. "Arletta!"

"I just have to tell you how smooth things are going with Mom. I just can't believe how happy she is, too. She's made some friends with those Angels, and some-times I think she'd rather see them than me." She snorted a laugh as she dug in her purse for something.

"I'm happy everything is going so well for you both.

So, now that things have settled maybe we can go get that lunch?"

"This is for you." Arletta handed her a white envelope.

"For me?" Lucy hesitantly took it.

"Open it now, or later. It doesn't matter. It's just a little something."

"Oh, you shouldn't have. I was just being … neighborly."

"It's from Mom. I told her all about you. She'd like to meet you one of these days." Arletta flashed a wide grin.

Lucy stepped forward and wrapped her arms around Arletta. "Thank you. Please tell your mom thank you, too. And yes, a visit to meet her sounds great."

"Well, gotta run. I have to get ready for my date."

"Date?"

"He's a cutie and wears a uniform like your Sam." Arletta's eyes twinkled when she spoke about him.

"Have fun. Don't do anything I wouldn't do," Lucy chimed.

She looked up to the brilliant blue sky with a just a couple of puffy clouds drifting through, and shook her head a couple of times. She drew in the sweet smell of the fall harvest, making her mouth water for tree ripened apples, squash, and more. The hot blistering temperatures of August were just a faded memory.

CHAPTER 16

With great concentration, she cut the carrots on the diagonal as the recipe called for, then cubed the potatoes, leaving on some of the skin as it contained most of the nutrition, and cut the onions in large chunks. She lowered the pork loin roast into the glass baking dish, seasoned it as directed, and then placed all the vegetables around it, finally placing the loaded dish into the preheated oven to do its magic. She hoped it would turn out as tasty as the reviewers said, and look as appetizing as the picture. She took out the frozen dessert to thaw. Not everything would be home-made on this first dinner, and it really bugged her, too. She opened the cellophane bag and took out some rolls, wrapping them up in foil. They'd go in last. She wiped her hands on the one apron she owned and smiled at a job well done. *Roast, check; veggies, check; rolls, check; dessert, check.* "I think that's it." She untied her apron and neatly hung it over the kitchen chair. "Oh, the wine!"

She brought down two wine glasses from the cabinet, selected a bottle from the small wrought iron rack that sat in the corner of her counter, and then took out the corkscrew. She'd let Sam have the honors. Now, she was ready!

She didn't have to wait for him long; soon there was a light tap at her front door. She swore she could smell his sweet self before he even stepped foot inside.

"Hey," she said, her eyes lighting up when she saw the beautiful bouquet he held.

"For you." He kissed her, then handed her the flowers.

"Thank you! I'll put these in water. Would you like to open the wine?" She led him to the small kitchen. "I don't own a vase … I've never received flowers before so never thought to buy one …" she murmured, looking inside the cabinets.

"Oh, man, I should have purchased the bouquet that came in a vase. I'm sorry, Lucy."

Pop went the sound of the cork.

"No worries, but let's see if I can improvise." She pulled out an empty mayonnaise jar from the recycle bin and held it up. "This should do."

Sam stepped closer to her. "It looks so clean."

"I washed it."

"You washed out the jar before you recycled it?"

"I know. I'm a little …"

"A little?" He chuckled.

"I'll be right back."

Lucy rushed to her spare bedroom. She reached for a small plastic container from the top shelf of the closet and rummaged through it. Locating what she'd been looking for, she closed the lid and put the container back on the shelf.

Sam watched her as he sipped his wine.

"Ta-da!" She whirled around and in her hand was the once plain jar now wrapped in a satin purple ribbon with the flowers.

"Wow, Lucy, that looks great. You must add flower arranging to your talents." He held up his wine glass in honor of her beautiful arrangement.

She strutted over to her small dining room table and slid the candles out of the way to put the flowers in the middle. "Now, that's a beautiful table." She crossed her arms as she admired her creativeness.

Sam handed her a glass of wine. "Let's sit. I've missed seeing you. Do we have time before dinner? And by the way, it smells really good."

She took his hand and led him to the sofa. "Yes, we

have about half an hour. And thank you. I hope you like pork loin."

"I love food, in general. How long have you known me?" he teased.

Shrugging, she drew in her bottom lip then took a sip of her wine.

"What was that for?" He tipped his chin toward her.

"I guess, I realized I haven't really known you for that long. If I did, maybe I'd know you love to eat, and that you do like pork roast." She closed her eyes and gave her head a slow dramatic shake.

"Now, Lucy, you know that was a rhetorical question. Don't take everything so darn seriously." He reached for her hand and laced his fingers with hers.

She peered up at him. Did he realize, even for a second, just how much he tortured her with his handsome good looks, piercing blue eyes, and sexy dimples? She inched closer.

He stared at her then smiled slowly, leaning in to meet her mouth.

A sexy beam pulled at her lips in anticipation of the kiss. He slid his hands around her neck and ran his fingers through her hair. "I'm glad you didn't cut your hair," he said through bated breath.

Nodding, she moved in closer to him. She could feel

the warmth of his breath as she inched even closer. She could not get enough of this man. "Sam?"

He trailed kisses down her neck, nibbled on her earlobe, and then moved to her mouth. "Uh-huh," was all he managed to say.

She closed her eyes and enjoyed each and every touch, forgetting what she was about to ask him. "Never mind," she responded as she tossed her head back and bit her lip to keep quiet as he dropped more kisses on her.

"I've missed you so much … your taste … your touch." He pressed his mouth to hers before she could answer.

She relaxed and gave in, giving him full access to her. She traced the muscles up his arms as he kissed her, playing with her in every fashion imaginable. She cupped his face, moving her hands around to the back of his neck, tasting him with her tongue as she kissed him back.

Buzz. Buzz.

They pulled apart.

"Dinner is ready." She jumped out of his embrace and moved to the kitchen.

HE LEANED BACK and palmed his stomach. "This was so good, Lucy."

"Glad you enjoyed it." She reached over and took his empty plate.

"Hey, I ate every crumb. That plate is so clean, you don't even have to wash it," he chortled.

Lucy drew her brows up.

"Just kidding."

"Are you ready for dessert?" Lucy stacked the dishes in the sink for later, and ran some water over them. Right now, all her attention would be on Sam. She'd try hard not to think about the drying food on the plates.

"What did you whip up? Let me guess, homemade cheesecake? No, maybe German chocolate cake, because that's one of my favorite desserts, or how about apple pie with a generous scoop of vanilla bean ice cream, another one of my favorites." His eyes were wide with eagerness.

"Well, sorry, Sam. Hate to break it to you, but it's none of those." She lowered her eyes.

"I'm sure whatever you made will be delicious," he said, trying to recover from his over presumptuous predictions of dessert.

"Actually, I didn't make dessert. Mrs. Smith did."

He opened his arms wide. "Hey, that's okay. I love Mrs. Smith desserts. We have them all the—"

"All the time? Were you going to say you have them all the time?" She leaned back in his arms.

His sheepish grin gave him away.

"At the firehouse," she said, nodding.

"Yeah, we do some cooking, and Scotty can bake some mean chocolate chip cookies, but for the most part, we do whatever is easiest." He lowered her onto his lap.

She laced her hands around his neck. "Okay, that makes me feel a bit better. Next time you come over, I'll have a homemade dessert. I promise." She kissed his nose.

"So, what did Mrs. Smith make for us?" He smiled and those cute little dimples popped right out.

"Banana cream pie."

His smile quickly became a frown.

"What? You don't like banana cream pie?" She leaped off his lap and crossed her arms, a frightful look appearing on her face.

"It's not that I don't like it. I'm allergic to bananas."

She grabbed her face with both hands. "See? We really don't know each other," she cried.

He took her hands away from her face and held them. "It's okay, Lucy. Rome wasn't built in a day. Let's go over to the sofa with our wine and talk."

"Talk? That's hard to do with you."

"What? You don't think I'm approachable? I can't carry on a decent conversation?" He led her to the couch and they both sat.

"No, I didn't mean it like that. It's just that when I get this close to you, I want to do anything but talk."

He tossed his head back and laughed. "Oh, I get it. I'm too irresistible. Yeah," he palmed his chest, "the ladies have a hard time keeping their hands to themselves." His sexy grin grabbed her heart and tugged hard.

"Sam Lyons, be serious," she said, showing him her puppy dog look.

"Let's play a little game. I'm going to ask you some questions, and then you'll ask me some. Ready?"

Their get to know you game revealed a lot about each of them. She found out his favorite color was green, his first car was a 1993 Camry, his favorite food was pepperoni pizza, and he loved to watch re-runs of old spaghetti westerns starring Clint Eastwood. Midnight, his first dog, a black Lab, still made him tear up when he talked about him, and his first career choice, to join the military, took a different turn when he joined the fire department as a volunteer. They'd already established that his favorite dessert was German chocolate cake, but she also learned that in addition to bananas, Sam also didn't like raw tomatoes, just like she didn't.

"I guess BLTs are out of the question for you," she teased.

"I just say hold the T." He laughed.

"I don't like the texture, for some reason," she said, shaking her head.

"But you know what's weird? I love fried green tomatoes." He closed his eyes and rocked his head back and forth as he recalled how much he liked them.

She openly shared with him her fear of falling short of always being perfect, her dislike for those who abused children and animals, her obsession with popcorn and M&M's, and the biggie, falling prey to men who wouldn't treat her right.

"First of all, there is only one perfect person, and you aren't him." He lowered his chin and nodded. "I hate those who abuse innocent children and animals, and I'd add another group to that list, the elderly."

"Oh, my, yes." Her eyes widened, realizing she'd forgotten to add the elderly, especially after everything she'd helped Arletta with. "I can't believe I forgot that one."

"I love a good batch of popcorn dripping in butter, and I like anything chocolate, so we're compatible, for sure." He winked.

When the second bottle of wine came out, they finished their game and decided to snuggle for the remainder of the evening. But just like she'd admitted to him earlier, once she was in his arms, all bets were off.

And she was right. But this time, he was the first one to give in.

"I love you, Lucy," he said in her ear as he moved over her, taking her breath away.

"I love you, too." She scooted down, resting her head on one of the sofa pillows. She traced his square jaw with her fingers and then ran them along his soft lips … the same lips she'd kissed many times but never got tired of. He nipped at her fingers and made her squeal, and then in one very calculated movement, he pressed his lips to hers. She moaned softly. His fingers threaded through her long locks, heightening her desire for more. She moved her hands over his protective arms, tempted by the softness of his skin, yet awed by his strength. When his mouth covered hers, she opened for him, his tongue dipping in where he was most welcomed, her soft tongue lashing back as if to say *hello, please stay awhile.*

And for a while, he stayed.

CHAPTER 17

"Someone sure is happy today." Pete slapped Sam on the back and then chuckled.

"Did Sam have a date with Lucy?" Scotty chimed in.

"Okay, guys, knock it off." Sam lugged the big black duffle bag with his change of clothes and headed toward the sleeping quarters.

"Oh, yeah, he's got it bad," Scotty said. "Whenever they won't kiss and tell then you know it's something special. Ain't that right, Sam?"

Sam raised his hand, squeezing his thumb with the rest of his fingers, giving them the yappy sign and kept walking.

The guys chuckled, happy to tease him unmercifully.

Sam settled into his side of the room he shared with Scotty. He hoped Scotty wouldn't keep on about Lucy.

He could take a lot of ribbing from the guys, and to be fair, he'd dished out a lot in the past, before they got married. It was only fair that he got his share of the teasing now.

He unpacked his few items and then headed back out to the main living area of the firehouse. Something smelled pretty good.

He lifted the lid on the huge pot and peered inside. He took a long and deep whiff of the bubbling concoction. Scotty could sure make a mean pot of stew. He lowered the lid and walked over to the fridge to peek inside. He chuckled quietly as he viewed the contents. Lucy had informed him she didn't like pickles. He counted three jars of various flavors. He grabbed a bottle of water and headed out to the garage. He took a deep breath. "Let the ribbing begin," he said under his breath.

"Hey, lover boy, so glad you could join us." Scotty flashed a wide grin.

"Come on, guys, give it a rest."

"Nope. Not until you tell us," Pete said, running a soft cloth across one of the truck's bumper.

"Tell you what?" Sam crossed his arms in defiance.

"Did you tell her that you love her and you couldn't live without her?" Pete teased.

"Okay, let me get this out in the open, once and for all. I know how you guys love paybacks."

Scotty and Pete nodded exaggeratedly.

"Yes, I told her that I love her. Yes, we had a great date. Yes, I think she's the one, and yes, yes, yes." Sam dropped his hands and shrugged. "What can I say? I'm crazy about Lucy."

Scotty waltzed over and laid his hand on Sam's shoulder. "Welcome to the club, son."

"Club?" Sam wrinkled his nose.

"The club of you'll never be right, so don't even try. Get familiar with the clerk over in the florist section of the grocery store. You'll be there a lot. Roses are the best and say I'm sorry, I love you, and more." Scotty raised his brows almost to his hairline, then gave a mild slap to Sam's back and walked away.

He couldn't imagine Lucy and him having that many arguments that would require him to buy flowers. Right now, when they had a little spat, they made up with hot steamy kisses and lots of *I'm sorry* whispered in one another's ears. He shook his head. "You guys have been married too long. We don't need flowers. We have each other."

Pete and Scotty exchanged surprised looks.

"It's already started, Scotty," Pete said with alarm in his voice.

"I know, Pete. I can't bear to watch." Scotty gasped and covered his eyes.

Then Pete and Scotty fell out laughing and soon Sam laughed right along with them.

They finished cleaning all the vehicles then chowed down on hot stew and corn bread. After dinner, the crew worked out in their makeshift gym, lifting weights, riding the stationary bike, and using the treadmill. After Sam worked up quite a sweat, he hit the shower, and then settled in one of the comfortable recliners to watch a little television before heading to bed.

At precisely 9:00 p.m., he called Lucy.

"I was beginning to think you weren't going to call."

"I told you I would call, silly," he said, trying to calm her worrying.

"I know. How was your day?" she asked.

"Good. Busy. I got teased by Pete and Scotty so much today."

"Teased? About what?"

He paused. Maybe he shouldn't have said anything. This was, after all, a guy thing. "Oh, nothing, just some guy stuff." He could think fast even lying down.

"I saw Arletta today. She's a new person. I'm not sure how I feel about it all."

"Why is that?" He turned over onto his side, trying to keep his eyes open while she talked.

"She went from being so negative to being very positive. And now she's dating a cop. So there's that, too."

She laughed into the phone, making him open his eyes. He'd drifted off to sleep. "Oh, okay," he said.

"Oh, okay? Is that all you have to say?"

"I'm sorry, Lucy. I'm beat. We polished all the trucks and I worked out. I'll call you tomorrow and we can talk when I'm not dozing off to sleep with the phone to my ear."

"That's fine. Call me tomorrow, then. Good night."

He may have been drowsy but he could hear how she was upset from her voice. He didn't want to end it that way. "Honey, you know I love you, right?"

"Do you?"

He shot straight up, pounding his head against the headboard. "What's that supposed to mean?"

"I don't know why I said that. Of course, I know you love me. I'm feeling needy, that's all." She hated the whiny self-absorbed sound of her voice.

"Hey, how's the class going? Any new art projects happening?" He knew he needed to change the trajectory of this conversation and quickly.

She spoke nonstop for the next five minutes in her most bubbly tone, telling him about the terrariums they were making, and the birdhouses out of milk jugs.

He smiled as he listened. "Sounds great, honey. Can't wait to see them."

"Open house is in two weeks. I hope you'll come."

"Give me the date tomorrow and I'll make sure I'm not working."

"Or covering someone's shift," she added.

"Or working an overtime shift for someone. Got it." He laughed. "Good night."

"Good night, Sam."

He tossed the phone onto the darkly stained nightstand and then slid down under the lightweight blanket. He tried to remember what her mouth felt like on his, and how her body made him feel when pressed tightly up against his. The next thing he knew he was waking up to the smell of freshly brewed coffee and bacon, another of Scotty's specialties.

He stumbled into the kitchen to find Pete and Scotty sitting around the Formica topped dinette set, sipping coffee and chowing down on breakfast.

"Good morning, sleepyhead." Pete watched as Sam poured his first cup of coffee before joining them at the table.

Sam scratched his head and then ran his hand along his chin. It reminded him to shave, but Lucy had once commented that she liked the feel of his stubble.

"What's on the agenda for today, Chief?" Sam drew in a taste of the hot coffee while locking eyes with Scotty.

"We're going to take engine number two out to the flats and do some training."

Sam tipped his head. "Okay, sounds good." He scooted his chair back and peered toward the stove. "Did you guys save me any breakfast?" He twisted back around and waited for either of them to reply.

"You know what time breakfast is." Scotty's face appeared so serious.

"Really? You didn't save me any bacon or eggs?" Sam crossed over to the kitchen, resolved to the fact that he'd have to have cold cereal. Then he spotted the plate covered with foil. He lifted a corner and found scrambled eggs and two pieces of bacon. He raised his head and smiled. The teasing would not stop this entire three-day shift. He picked up the plate and made his way back to the table.

"Hey, there, looks like you're trying to grow some grass on your face." Scotty motioned toward the almost three days of growth on his face.

"I'll shave this morning. It's just that—"

"Lucy loves to run her fingers through your stubble," Pete sang, making Scotty chuckle and Sam narrow his eyes.

"I'll shave it this morning." Sam dug into his room temperature eggs and chewed quickly, not making eye contact with either of them. He'd had enough of them.

∽

THE CREW of three participated in readiness exercises, which constituted them each carrying a heavy pack with water and hand tools, a hydration water pack, which also held more water and their radios. In addition to endurance training, they practiced cutting lines through thick brush for access to a scenario of wildfires burning acres beyond. They also practiced wrapping in sheltering material, which any of them would tell you they hoped they'd never have to use.

Sam swung his hatchet as he cut through thick brush, making a path. Carrying the load on his back of almost seventy-five pounds, he'd worked up quite a sweat. Stopping for just a moment, he wiped the beads from his brow and drew water from the built-in straw of the water pack he carried.

He'd just taken a step when he heard the rattle. "Snake," he called, lowering his hatchet in one quick move.

Pete came up behind him when he heard the call. "Looks like you got him good." He patted Sam on the back.

"Snakes."

A puzzled look appeared on Pete's face. "What?"

"Snakes—I forgot to add that I have a fear of snakes to my list."

Pete shook his head. "Have you been out in the sun

too long? You're not making any sense. Drink some more water."

"No." Sam laughed. "We were playing a game where we told each other what we liked and didn't like. I forgot to tell Lucy that I was afraid of snakes."

"Afraid or just don't like them? There is a differ-ence." Pete shifted his pack on his back and then laced his hands through the straps against his chest.

"I don't like them *and* I'm afraid of them."

"Okay, my friend. So what else did you learn about Lucy?" They continued cutting their path.

"Her favorite color is purple and she loves popcorn." Sam stopped. "You didn't really want to know this, right?" He drew his lips tight and twisted them to the left.

Pete made a funny cross-eyed face with his tongue hanging out. "Not really, but it's nice to know she loves popcorn, cuz when you two are snuggled up on the couch watching love movies, you can nibble on something besides her ear." He reared his head back and laughed.

Sam shook his head briskly. When would he ever learn this bunch loved to get into his head!

After a very long day they headed back to the station.

Inside the rig it was loud. Everyone had to yell to hear one another.

"It's your turn to cook tonight," Pete shouted.

He drew in a deep breath and blew it out slowly. He

was not the best cook at the station and everyone knew that. Scotty had that honor. They also knew that when it was Sam's turn it was usually hot dogs and beans.

"At least grill the hot dogs." Scotty winked at Sam.

He chuckled. They knew him so well.

CHAPTER 18

"Lucy," Arletta said, greeting her as she opened the door and welcoming her in.

"Hey." Lucy stepped inside.

"So glad you could make it. Mom asked if you were coming." She motioned toward the back of the house.

"I had a couple of errands to run after class. How are you?" She followed Arletta.

"I'm good."

Lucy stopped in her tracks. "Just good? Where did great, fantastic, and nothing could be better go?"

"I'll tell you about that later. Hey, Mom, here's Lucy …"

Lucy and Arletta laughed out loud when they heard *here's Lucy*. It reminded them of the movie *The Shining* when Jack Nicholson says, "Here's Johnny."

Lucy hurried over to the overstuffed chair where Arletta's mother sat. A quilt lay across her lap and on the quilt rested a Bible.

"Hello, Mrs. Bryon. It's nice to meet you." Lucy held out her hand.

"Thank you so much for helping my Arletta figure out some things with my care. It's made such a difference. I have so many nice young people who come visit me now. I just love it."

"Well, you're very welcome. I'm glad I could help." Lucy offered a warm smile to the ailing Mrs. Bryon.

"Please have a seat," Mrs. Bryon said.

Lucy sat for about thirty minutes and listened to several old stories that brought light to Mrs. Bryon's eyes. She found it quite interesting about her past and enjoyed that it brought the older lady so much joy in reliving and retelling the tales.

"Well, I better get going. It's getting late and you should rest." Lucy stood.

"I'll walk you out." Arletta hadn't spoken a word since Lucy sat down and visited with her mom.

The two women stood outside.

"Your mom seems to be adjusting well to all the new visitors. Sometimes it can be a bit overwhelming. Old people are so set in their ways." She focused on Arletta's eyes.

"Yeah, she's been a trooper about it," she said, choking out the last bit.

"What's wrong, Arletta?" Lucy recognized the hitch of pain in her friend's voice.

"I thought everything was going so good, and then he just said he wanted space."

Lucy rolled her bottom lip in. "Sometimes they say it because they are scared of how close they are getting. They can't sort out all their feelings. It's new to them."

Arletta crossed her arms. "Maybe. But the way he just abruptly said it, I don't know. Could be there is someone else."

"Now, Arletta, why would you think that?"

"I don't know. Maybe because I'm not worthy of being someone's girlfriend."

"Arletta, you know that's not true. Now you're beginning to sound like the old me."

She uncrossed her arms and let them loosely dangle by her sides. "You?"

"Yep. I didn't think anyone would ever care about me because of my OCD, and my relationship issues. But then I met Sam, and all that changed."

"Sam's a great catch."

"Yes, and if your cop isn't, then there might be someone else better suited for you. My point is, don't give up, and don't beat yourself up over it. It really is his loss." Lucy narrowed her eyes. "Your mom sure is an inspiration." She tipped her head toward the closed door.

"I know. I have to keep telling myself that. If she can find joy and happiness while she's bound to the house pretty much, I don't have a darn thing to complain about."

"Well, we do have things to complain about. Don't oversimplify it, but we must really search our hearts before we judge and before we complain." Boy, would her dad be proud of her. "Anyway, keep your chin up. I have a feeling he might be calling you again. And when he does, take that opportunity to lay your cards out."

"Lucy, thanks for your wise words. You really are a breath of fresh air. No wonder Sam is so much in love with you."

Lucy shook her head slowly as a smile worked its way across her mouth. She couldn't believe how much she loved him, either. And to think it all started with an entry in a contest. She stepped away and crossed over to her parked car. As she opened the door, she looked up, flashing a quick wave goodbye.

"Lucy," Arletta shouted from the stoop.

Lucy shielded her eyes from the late afternoon sun as it moved across their roofline. "Yes?"

"One of these nights when Sam has to work, let's go out, just us girls. Dodge City is a wild and happening place on a Friday or Saturday night." She laughed loudly, her voice carrying to the car.

Lucy nodded. "Okay, it's a date." She slipped into her car and drove away.

She sat with her phone on her lap, waiting eagerly for her 9:00 p.m. phone chat with Sam. Right when it turned to nine, he called.

"Hello," she said on the first ring.

A low belly laugh echoed through the receiver. "Were you sitting on the phone?"

"I look forward to your calls." She wrapped a lock of hair around her finger and twirled it.

"I'm beat again tonight. We trained all day."

Hearing the tiredness in his voice, she grimaced. *Was it selfish of her to keep him on the line?* "I'm sorry you're so tired. We can talk tomorrow when I see you."

"Would you be too terribly upset with me if I told you I was working an overtime shift?"

"Sam!"

"Listen, I can explain. I want the day off to come to your open house. This is how I'll get it off. The schedule is already made up, so I switched with Tony."

"Tony? Who's Tony?" This was a new name for her.

"He's one of our part-time guys."

"Oh, I see. Okay. I really want you to be present at the open house."

"Love you, Lucy."

"Love you, too."

"Just think how much more intense our time together will be once we're together."

She liked the sound of that. Just thinking about his touch drove her wild. She sucked in a soft breath and then tried her best to conceal it as she exhaled. Her heart was beating like a jackhammer and he hadn't even touched her yet.

"GIRLS' night out, yeah," Arletta said, turning up the music.

Lucy widened her eyes as she watched her drive a little too erratically for her taste. "Can you slow down just a bit?"

With the music blaring inside the car, she ignored Lucy's pleas, but when the flashing blue lights and siren blasted from behind, Arletta quickly pulled the car over and came to a complete stop.

Lucy removed her death grip from the door. "Oh, great," is all she said.

Arletta reached across Lucy and retrieved the car registration from the glove box. She removed her driver's license from her wallet and rolled down the window. She gasped when she saw her former boyfriend.

She didn't wait for him to ask for her documents. She presented them to him as he aimed the flashlight into the car, blinding Lucy. He then turned the light onto the documents.

"You were driving a little fast there, Ms. Arletta Bryon."

Lucy watched in total amazement as the little charade played out before her. Was it good cop, bad cop, girlfriend, boyfriend, or something else happening here?

"We were on our way to the club. You know, the one we were supposed to go to, but never did." Arletta's tone bit sharply through the car, causing Lucy to shudder.

"No excuse for breaking the speed limit. I'll let you off with a warning this time. But next time … you won't be so lucky." He handed back her documents. She briskly took them out of his hand, making Lucy cringe once more over her friend's brusque behavior.

"I'm sorry, Officer. It won't happen again," Lucy said, trying to appeal to his good side. Surely he had one?

Arletta cut her eyes toward Lucy. "Don't tell him that," she snapped.

"Arletta," she whispered through gritted teeth. "Calm

down. He's letting you off with a warning." She folded her fingers in a wave toward the officer. "Have a great evening," she called out.

The cop walked back to his car. The two women fussed over the proper etiquette one should follow when being pulled over by a policeman for speeding. Finally, they both fell out laughing at how bizarre the entire thing really was.

Arletta looked back in her rearview mirror. "And he's driving away ..."

Lucy and Arletta watched as the police cruiser drove past them. They sat for a few more seconds before resuming their own travels.

"I say this calls for a little celebration." Arletta whipped the car back into the lane and sped toward the club.

"Haven't you learned a single thing tonight?" Lucy resumed her death grip on the door.

THEY FOUND a table in a back corner, and while Arletta went to the bar to get them each a drink, Lucy eyed the dance floor where flocks of young people danced. It made her think about Sam all the more when she saw couples slow dancing and sneaking in kisses.

"Here you go," Arletta said, setting a drink down before her.

"What is it?" Lucy eyed the red drink.

"I don't know. I just told him make it fruity and make it strong." Arletta drew a sip of her drink.

Lucy tipped her head toward the dance floor. "Watching all of them makes me want to have Sam."

"I can't believe that jerk."

Lucy shot her a nasty look. "What?"

"Oh, I meant Luke."

"Oh! For a minute, I thought you meant Sam."

"He tried to play like he didn't even know me. What's that about?"

"It's called he was doing his job. You were speeding." Showing her she was in the wrong, she tipped her head and pursed her lips tightly.

Arletta cupped her mouth and leaned forward. "You know what?" she whispered.

Lucy dipped her head. "What?"

"I did it on purpose. I know that's his area to nab speeders."

Lucy chuckled. "Well, you should be thankful that he didn't write you a ticket."

"Hey, girls, can we join you?" Two big guys approached their table, startling them.

The girls looked up then looked back at each other.

They stumbled a bit but then Arletta spoke. "Sorry, but these chairs are taken for our boyfriends."

The two men mumbled something under their breath and then quickly moved on.

"Our boyfriends?" Lucy took a sip of her drink.

"I think I need a makeover," Arletta announced, changing the subject.

"That's easy. We'll go to the store, buy a box of hair color, and I'll fix you right up."

"Let's blow this place. It's not what I was hoping for, anyway." Arletta scooted her chair back.

Lucy plunged her lips on the straw for one last draw of the tasty drink and then grabbed her purse.

THEY BOUGHT a bottle of wine and a box of hair color, and set off for Lucy's apartment where she promised to transform Arletta's mousy brown hair to something with copper highlights.

Lucy set up a makeshift beauty shop in her bathroom, but kept Arletta's back to the vanity. "Keep your eyes closed until I tell you," Lucy said when she was finally finished, gently turning Arletta around so she could see her new look in the mirror. "Okay, open them," she said as she placed her squarely in front of the large mirror, ready to hand her a small handheld mirror so she could see all sides of her new self.

Arletta covered her mouth to conceal her gasp. She just stood there staring at herself.

"Do you like it?"

She removed her hand and a couple of tears trailed down her cheeks. "I love it."

"Here's a mirror so you can see the back." Lucy twirled her around as she handed her the purple mirror.

"Lucy, this is so perfect. You can add beautician to your repertoire of professions. This is awesome." She fluffed up the back with her hand. "And the color—it's perfect."

"It's called sienna brown. It has some red highlights, which look really good with your skin tone and eye color."

"Love it," is all Arletta managed to say before she burst out crying.

"What's wrong? I thought you loved it?" Lucy pulled her in for a hug. "I can change the color, the length can grow back, I just thought this bob looked so cute on you," she said, rambling.

Arletta shook her head and then pulled out of the hug. "No, I don't want to change a thing. I really do love it."

"Then why the sobbing?"

"Because you made me beautiful."

"Oh, Arletta, I didn't make you beautiful! You already are. I just enhanced some of your features. It was always here. You have to believe in yourself, too." Taking her finger, she lifted her chin. "I'm glad you love the new look. I think Luke will, too."

Arletta's eyes lit up. "Do you think so?"

"If he doesn't, then he's one blind cop."

*L*ucy had to strain to hear him, his tired voice was barely above a whisper. Waiting until he finished, she replied, "I can't wait to see you."

"After tonight, I'm off for the next four days. Give me a day to feel human again, and then I'll be right over to see you."

"Oh, Sam, do I have to wait that long?" She purred into the phone, trying to stir something … anything in her tired fireman.

"I promise the wait will be worth it." His sexy voice came in loud and clear.

She could feel the warmth travel to her face as she tried to steady her voice before replying. "Okay," she mumbled.

After they hung up, Lucy remembered so many things

she had wanted to tell him. But it was no use. He'd probably not even remember them. His brain was fried from all the hours he'd been working.

TRYING to cope with her high levels of anxiety, and relieve the onslaught of tension she felt building in anticipation of the school open house, Lucy dropped her arms by her side, shrugging and shaking her hands while taking deep breaths. She looked up at the clock. Soon she'd have to put on her brave smile. She made her way through the rows of desks, making sure every desk had something of the child's to share with their parents. She walked over to the terrariums and smiled. Just then the classroom door opened and in walked Arletta.

"Hey, Arletta. What are you doing here?"

"I came to wish you good luck on your first open house." She held out a small bouquet of colorful flowers.

"Oh, you shouldn't have." She drew in a whiff of their fragrant scent. "Thank you."

"I won't stay, but I just wanted to also tell you that Luke and I have a date tonight." She rocked back and forth on her heels and smiled.

"Oh, that's great! Keep me posted." She winked at her friend.

"Is Sam coming tonight?"

Not letting on that Sam's absence disappointed her, she sugarcoated his excuse to Arletta. "He's exhausted. He finished the last of his forty-eight-hour shift this morning. He said he needed a day to feel normal again before I'd see him."

Arletta tipped her forehead. "Okay, well knock 'em dead, or whatever it is you teachers do to parents on open house night." She laughed as she made her way to the door. Just then, the door opened and several eager parents flew in.

"Bye," Arletta mouthed as she zigzagged around them.

Lucy made eye contact with a set of parents and crossed over to them. She chatted a few moments and then moved on to the next set of parents to come through the door. Soon, a steady stream of parents came and went over the next hour. She enjoyed meeting them all, and although she made a point to acknowledge the individuality of her students, after meeting their parents, she had to admit that even at this young age, the apple hadn't fallen far from the tree.

She looked over her sign-up sheet and all but two parents had showed. She'd give them a few more minutes before cleaning up. At eight o'clock, she began to box up the leftover chocolate chip cookies, gather the unused napkins and the lemonade punch she'd made, and placed them in her cooler with wheels. She walked over to the desk and retrieved her purse from the drawer, and then pulling the cooler, she made her way to the door. Just then, it flew open and an out of breath Sam ran in. "Am I late?" His eyes darted around the room. "I lay down for just a few minutes, but I must have dozed off. I'm sorry if I'm late."

Lucy's breath hitched as she studied him. He made it. She didn't care if he only had minutes to spare, he made it. He came through for her without her reminding him. She stepped closer toward him. "Sam, I love you." She walked into his arms and held him tightly.

He chuckled. "Aren't you going to show me around the classroom?"

"Yes, but I want to hold you for a minute. I missed you."

He rocked her in his arms, dropping a kiss on the top of her head. His concentration broke when he heard the classroom door open.

"Ms. Carmichael?" a voice asked.

Lucy let go of Sam and moved him out of the way. Her eyes landed on a balding man dressed in jeans and a white work shirt with a logo sewn on the pocket. She extended her hand. "Yes, I'm Ms. Carmichael."

"I'm sorry I'm late. I had to work late, but Jason

wouldn't have understood me missing meeting you. That's all he talks about." His eyes twinkled, softening her heart.

"Well, let's see. Let me show you where Jason sits and some of the stuff he's been working on." She looked over her shoulder at Sam as she walked with Jason's dad to the middle section of the desks. While she explained a few things to Jason's dad, her eyes traveled with Sam as he meandered through the classroom looking at different things.

After the five-minute tour, Jason's dad left with a packet of art work and other school work.

"You were so great with that dad. He really appreciated that you took the time to show him his son's work, even though it was past the time."

"I love being a teacher, and whenever I can share a child's work, be it creativity, science, or math, I'm always excited to bring a smile to the parents' faces. It always does, too. Let's go," Lucy said, reaching for the cooler handle.

Sam took it from her and motioned with his head for her to lead the way. She turned the lights off to the classroom, and then holding hands they walked down the hallway with the shiny waxed floors glistening under the bright lights.

He set the cooler inside her trunk, and then with her

back against the car, he took her hands in his. "I'm sorry I was late." He circled her thumbs with his.

"I don't care. You came and that's all that really matters."

"You did a great job for the open house."

"Oh," she said, now circling his thumbs with hers. "What did you like most about it?" she teased, putting him on the spot.

"I like how colorful it is, with so many things to look at. And the projects … you keep those kids busy. No wonder they need a nap." He chuckled then squeezed her hands.

Not wanting to address the nap thing again, she playfully ignored it by giggling. "Can you come back to my place and visit for a bit?"

He pulled her in, answering her with a wink. Then he closed his mouth on hers, and all she wanted to do was enjoy his warm kiss.

SHE RUSHED AROUND, pulling on her one shoe and then the other before running out of the bedroom. Opening the fridge, her eyes landed on a carton of yogurt and some bologna. She quickly made herself a lunch and then tossed it inside her thermal lunch bag. She pulled her purse off of the chair and searched for her keys. Just as she was about to fly out the door, she reached up and touched her ears. *"Grr."*

She ran back into the bedroom and rummaged through her jewelry box, settling on gold hoops. *They go with everything.* Convinced she looked like someone who had overslept, she ran out the door to head to class, hoping the children wouldn't notice.

She had five minutes to spare before the bell went off. She smiled when she thought about Sam. Oversleeping and almost being late to work was *so* worth it.

Lucy, extremely hungry for lunch, couldn't wait for the clock to strike eleven thirty. She quickly grabbed her lunch bag and hurried to the teachers' lounge. She tore into her bologna sandwich, taking a bite as she crossed her legs. She looked down at her dark blue shoe. She could have sworn she'd worn black shoes. Then she uncrossed her legs and looked at her other foot. Her eyes widened in horror. She had two different colored shoes on today! She nibbled on her sandwich, keeping her feet tucked under the table so that no one would notice. She looked down at the rest of her clothing, wondering what else she may have missed in her quick attempt to get dressed. She wrapped her sandwich back up and put it away. She'd lost any appetite she'd had.

As soon as class was dismissed, she bolted out of

school and headed home. The more she thought about the mismatched shoes, the more she found it funny. *So what? I wore different colored shoes.* But when she reached back and felt a big knotted bulge on the back of her head, she freaked out again. "Geeze. Can I catch a break here?"

Standing at her front door, she dug in her purse for her keys when her phone started ringing. She wondered if Sam would find it amusing about her dressing debacle.

It was Arletta. She stuck the key in her apartment door lock and turned the knob. "Hey, Arletta." She held the phone against her face with her shoulder.

"I just had to tell you about my date last night."

Lucy shut the door with her foot and tossed her purse over the chair. "How was it?"

"Great. Fantastic."

"Great and fantastic? Wow. Never thought I'd hear you say those two words." She chuckled as she made her way into the kitchen. Feeling famished, she started searching for something easy to make to go along with her half-eaten sandwich.

"He loved my new look. He couldn't stop talking about it."

"I'm so happy, Arletta." She grabbed the carton of eggs. All of a sudden, bologna didn't appeal to her.

"We already have another date. He wants to take me away for the weekend."

Lucy paused. A weekend getaway sounded delightful. She and Sam could use one of those. "Have a great time."

"Maybe we could double date sometime. With Luke being a policeman and Sam a fireman, they'd have some stuff in common, don't you think?"

"I think that would be awesome, except I can hardly get a single date out of that man, let alone a double. But I'll work on it. It does sound fun. We could take them to that club you and I went to."

"You work on Sam, and I'll keep the flames burning with old Luke. When the time is right, we'll go boogying." Arletta laughed in the phone, bringing a smile to Lucy's face.

"Sounds great, Arletta. I'm going to let you go before I burn my eggs, okay?"

She sat down and dug in to her overcooked eggs and slightly burnt toast. She'd just forked a bit of her eggs and was about to take a bite, when her phone rang again. The caller ID told her it wasn't Arletta forgetting to tell her something, but the love of her life, Sam!

She pushed the plate away and sat back deep into the chair. "Hello, baby," she cooed.

"How's my sweetheart?" His tone, chipper and bright, brought a smile to her face.

"I'm well. I had a rough start this morning, though. I

wore two different colored shoes to school today." She giggled at the recollection.

He roared into the phone. "How'd you do that?"

"Someone made me late this morning. In my rush to get out the door, I put on two different colors. Thankfully, they were navy blue and black, but I could tell. Then, to top it off, I didn't get all the tangles out of my hair."

"Hmm. Well, that does present a problem. Maybe I need to come over so we can practice again … you know, just so you'll be ready to make a mad dash out the door to class."

She couldn't help it. His humor made her smile. "Don't tempt me, Sam Lyons."

"I'm being serious. I want to see you again tonight." His sexy voice made her quiver.

"Okay. You know I'm always happy to see you." She cringed at the corniness of her reply.

"I want you to come over to my place tonight. Okay?"

"By the way, Arletta bounced an idea around about us double dating. Thought it sounded fun if we can get you two community service employees off on the same day. I think Luke works a crazy schedule like you do."

"Okay, that sounds good. Luke is good people," Sam said.

Lucy switched the phone to her other ear. "You know Luke?"

"The service community is small, Lucy. We know all the cops here."

"Oh, I guess I should have known that. I'm glad to hear he's good people. My only experience with him was when he pulled us over for speeding."

Sam chuckled. "He probably did that on purpose because of Arletta."

"That's what I told her."

"Anyway, can't wait to see you, babe." His soft-spoken, sexy voice caused the hair on the back of her neck to crawl, making her shudder.

She tossed her head back and sighed as she remembered his warm, sweet kisses. "Me, either," she whispered.

HE OPENED the door and let her inside. "Now, I want you to know that I cleaned up my apartment because I didn't want you to see how messy I really can be."

Her eyes traveled around the small apartment. Standing in the middle of the living room her eyes got a glimpse into his bedroom and the nearby kitchen. If you could call it a kitchen. It was more like a galley. "You did a great job." She didn't have the heart to tell him she could see the toes of several pairs of shoes under his bed, or the wadded-up tee shirt sticking out from under the sofa cushion. It didn't really matter. She'd take him with all of his messiness.

"I made us dinner, too." He crossed over to the kitchen.

"Something smells delicious." She wasn't lying, either. It really did.

"I'm not known for my cooking skills, but Pete and Scotty have taught me a few things." He lifted the lid and took a whiff. He shook his head and started to replace the lid.

She slipped her hand on top of his, halting him from covering the pan. She leaned in and whiffed as well. "Oh, man, that smells so good."

"It's called goulash. I made rice to pour it over, too."

She admired his efforts. He had even tried to set the table properly, including candles in the middle. When dinner was over with, he led her to the couch where he served her coffee and warm chocolate chip cookies, which were slice and bake from the grocery store, but delicious nonetheless.

"This has been wonderful. Thank you." She sat back deep into the cushions and relaxed her shoulders. "I love just being here with you. It's so nice." She laced her hand through his arm.

"I was wondering how you'd feel about a weekend getaway?" She nuzzled closer to him.

"Okay, I'll have to look at my schedule."

"Nothing too far away, but somewhere romantic." She lifted her chin and waited.

He looked at her with half-closed lids and then leaned in for a kiss, searching for something deeper than the quick kiss they'd shared earlier. She groaned, softly stirring him to pleasure her more with his sensual kisses.

Catching their breath, they stayed cuddled on the sofa, and in between hot kisses, made plans for the future. It always gave her hope this relationship would stand the test of time and weather any bumps due to all the hours he spent away for his job, especially when they discussed their future.

"We have a huge Thanksgiving dinner at the fire station. I hope you'll come."

"I promised my folks I'd come home." She pouted.

"What if I share you?"

"Share me?" She titled her head and gave him a puzzled look.

"I get you for Thanksgiving and they can have you for Christmas."

She drew her finger to her mouth and tapped it. "Hmm. Let me see. What will you do to make it worth me asking them?" Her sexy bravado turned him on.

He pulled her on top of him and scooted down, resting his head on the arm of the couch. "Girl, you make me want to—"

"Do what?" she teased, running her tongue across her lips.

"Do this." He covered her mouth and dipped his tongue between her lips. He ran his hand up under her blouse, feeling her flesh. She ran her hands through his thick hair, sending shivers down his spine and everywhere else.

IF ONLY SHE knew how she totally affected him. He thought about her all the time. He even found himself thinking about her when he was fighting fires—something they've been trained not to do. He couldn't help it. He wanted to see her more, develop their relationship better, but it seemed his job always interfered. She never once complained, though. Not too much, anyway. He laid his hand on her leg and ran it up and down the length of her thigh.

CHAPTER 20

The school year moved along and Lucy settled right in with her new class and new school district. Her fellow teachers, principal, and other staff all welcomed her with open arms, and soon her classroom in Denver was all but a fleeting thought. Her time with Sam became more consistent, too, and soon they were spending every waking—and non-waking—moment they could with one another. She was so much in love it made her head spin.

Fall, definitely in the air, brought with it the crisp cool temperatures she loved. Day trips to the farmers' market, exploring the eighty-acre lake nearby, and looking up at the stars on a chilly night, wrapped up in his arms, kept them busy, but not necessarily out of trouble. She pulled her finger to her lips and touched them, recalling how his mouth felt on hers. Can this really be happening?

She tossed in the homemade pimento cheese, sliced sourdough bread, pickles (because he loved them), and oversized oatmeal cookies freshly baked the evening before. She made sure she packed some plastic utensils, napkins, and the super cute wine glasses made of acrylic she'd found at a local crafting store, along with a bottle of their favorite wine. Today, he was taking her somewhere special he said. Somewhere they'd never been before. She hunched her shoulders then relaxed them. Any place with him would be just fine with her. She looked one last time inside the deep woven basket and then shut the lid.

A light rap at her front door brought a wide smile to her face. She hurriedly made her way to the door, eager to see Sam.

"Wow, don't you look nice," he said, placing both hands on her arms as he pulled her close for a kiss. "And smell good, too." He winked.

"Our picnic lunch is all packed." She motioned over to the brown basket sitting on the kitchen counter, but her eyes never wavered from his physique. Any excuse to look and drool, she took.

He crossed over to the basket and clenched it with his strong hands. "I'm super excited about where we are headed today." He led the way out the door.

"I love surprises." Her heart leaped just a tad knowing she'd be spending the entire day with him.

They drove for almost an hour, and she wondered if where they were headed was even in the state of Kansas. Finally, he pulled off the main road and took a dirt road lined with very old cottonwood trees. They bumped along the rocky dirt road until they came to a clearing. Turning, she looked over at Sam when they pulled up to an old fishing cabin.

He turned off the engine and sat a moment, taking it all in. "One of the retired fire chiefs owns this property. He stopped by the station last week to say hi and soon we were talking about his fishing cabin. He mentioned it wasn't getting used like it once was and if any of us wanted to use it, we could. I jumped at the opportunity." He exhaled a deep breath. "Isn't it so cool?" He turned toward her, a big smile on his face.

She nodded. "Well, I haven't seen the inside yet, but yes, the grounds are very nice."

"Let's go." He popped open the door and ran around to help her out. She still loved how he doted on her.

He grabbed the basket and a few other things from the back of his truck and led the way. He had to really push hard on the front door to get it to open. "It's a bit warped from the weather," he said, trying to remain optimistic that the fishing cabin was more than a shack.

Lucy's eyes grew wide when she stepped inside the dark and dank room. She sneezed.

"Bless you."

"I think this place requires a good cleaning." She walked over to the large window in the back of the room and threw open the curtains. A few ounces of dust went flying along with the bare thread material. She coughed.

"Come out here, Lucy."

She followed his voice to the back door and stepped out onto a large deck. She gasped when she saw the gorgeous view.

"This is Lake Charles."

"It's so calm and really pretty." She looped her arm in his.

"I haven't been up here to this lake in ages." He stared straight ahead, his voice as calm as the water. "There are trails that go around the lake. I thought maybe after lunch we could go exploring." He rested his hand on top of hers, holding her arm snug against his body.

She peered around him. "There's a table with chairs, so we can just sit outside."

After they enjoyed lunch, they took off into the woods, crunching along the earthy path with overgrown flora, and enjoying the fall air. With the sun just ever so lightly warming them, Lucy took off her zippered hooded sweatshirt and tied it around her waist. It was the best of both worlds. Stopping at every little cleared out area, most likely worn down from a deer or other large animal, they admired the lake from different perspectives. After walking for a good half-hour, they came upon a large clearing with a bench made out of crude pieces of lumber and sat down to rest with a perfect view of the lake.

"Oh, Sam, this is so beautiful. Thanks for bringing me here. It's like we're in another world or something." She snuggled into him, breathing in his warm scent.

"It's so peaceful. Would you stay up here sometime for a weekend?" He lowered his gaze to her.

Pausing just a moment, she said, "Only after a thorough cleaning." She laughed.

"Deal." He dropped a kiss on her head.

She straightened out of his hold and looked up. She wanted more than just a kiss on the head.

The kiss, already very passionate, seemed to be heightened by the outdoors. She wrapped her hands around his neck, holding him in place. They had some serious chemistry with or without the outdoors. She sighed softly when he moved away.

"Lucy?"

"Uh-huh." Her voice was low and soft.

"I know you and I have only been going out for a few months—"

"They've been the best few months of my life," she said, not letting him finish.

"Mine, too. You moved away from your family to be with me. I want you to know that's a big thing in my book."

"Quit my job I loved, moved away from my best friend …"

Sam pulled away and cocked his head. "Wait, Beth moved before you did."

Lucy giggled and then looped her arm with his again. "Just checking to see if you really listen to me."

"My point is, you've made a lot of sacrifices for me." His tone, steady and very serious, was making her take note.

She loosened her arm from his and studied his face, searching for answers. What was he about to tell her?

"I love you with all my heart." He dug inside the black and white plaid flannel shirt jacket he wore and produced a black velvet box. He popped open the top, exposing a shiny diamond ring. "Will you marry me?"

Lucy covered her mouth to hide her gasp. "Yes! Yes, I'll marry you." She held out her ring finger.

He carefully took the white gold band with diamonds and slid it onto her finger. He sighed. "A perfect fit." He leaned in and kissed her.

"Sam, I don't know what to say. I love you so very

much. This is the happiest day of my life. So, let me see. Today is October fifteenth. We got engaged on October fifteenth," she said, her voice rising each time she said it.

"When do you think we should have the wedding?" His eyes twinkled and she swore she saw a bit of moisture glistening in his eyes.

"Well, it won't be a large wedding. I don't know that many people—my parents for sure, your sister Wanda, your mom, the fire crew, of course, Beth and Caleb, oh, and Arletta and her boyfriend Luke."

"I'll leave the details up to you. I'm good with whatever you decide. We can even get married in Denver if you want." He held her hand close to his chest while he spoke.

A few tears rolled down her cheeks. "You'd agree to have the wedding in Denver? But all your friends are here."

"I'm just saying … whatever you want. I just want you to be Mrs. Lyons."

Her eyes widened. "Mrs. Lyons, Mrs. Samuel Lyons."

"Mrs. Lucille Lyons." His eyes drew her in.

Her hand flew to her mouth.

"What's wrong?"

"My initials—they will be LOL!" She broke out laughing.

"What's the O for? I know I probably should know this." His face turned red.

"Olivia."

"Samuel Paul Lyons, at your service." He bowed.

Lucy stood. Taking his hand, she urged him to stand. "We didn't cover that in the game we played." She laced her arms around his muscular waist.

"No, I guess not."

They held hands and walked the path back to the cabin. Along the way, they played round two of getting to know one another. They both laughed at the silliness of playing such a game after they got engaged, but as a teacher, Lucy reminded Sam learning something new each day could be very fulfilling.

"When did you kiss your first girl?"

He threw his head back and laughed. "I was eleven. It was behind the elementary school. How about you?"

"I was sixteen. It was at the school dance."

"Late bloomer, huh?" He knocked her shoulders with his.

"Sam?"

"Yep."

"Are you going to be okay with my OCD? I mean, I can be a bit overbearing when it comes to tidiness."

"You mean you won't want my white gym socks decorating the sofa anymore?" His teasing made her smile. "It will take some getting used to, but I think I can overcome it."

The rest of the afternoon, they played the get to know you game off and on. Convinced they'd never find out everything, even in a year, they moved on from that, although it was difficult for Lucy to give it a break. Her OCD kept rearing its head.

"Lucy, I thought we agreed. We're not going to know everything about one another before the wedding. Just chill."

She slumped in the passenger seat. "I just don't want any surprises, or to surprise you, for that matter."

"I don't care about your past. I love you in the present. Unless you're married to someone else and have a bunch of kids holed up somewhere, I'm satisfied I know you well enough to have you as my wife."

She rolled her head toward him. "You weren't married before, were you?"

"Lucille Carmichael, don't you think I'd have told you that?"

"Okay, I'll stop. Anyway, I can't wait to call my mom. She'll be so happy. She really likes you. And you know what else?" Her eyes glistened with a mischievous look.

He shrugged. "No, what else?"

"I don't normally like it when my folks call me

Lucille. But the way the letters roll off your tongue makes me feel safe and secure. Like you'll always be around and be my protector."

"I plan on it. And you know what else?"

Shaking her head, she hunched her shoulders.

"You don't cry nearly as much as you did when we first met and started dating. I'm really glad about that, too." He pulled his eyes from the road for a second and the corners of his mouth drew up.

She blew out the breath she'd been holding in anticipation of what he'd say. Less crying was a good thing. Any tears that flowed from her eyes from now on would be tears of joy. She reached over and placed her hand on his leg. "I love you, Sam."

He cupped her hand sending tingles all through her body. "I love you, too."

THE MICROWAVE BEEPED. Lucy shuffled into the kitchen and prepared her cup of tea. Plumping up the pillows on the couch, she settled in the corner, holding the tea to her lips and blowing on the hot beverage. After a few moments, she couldn't delay any longer. She picked up the phone and called her mom.

"Oh, my, Lucy, that's wonderful news! When's the wedding?"

Lucy giggled as she held the phone out from her mother's overly excited tenor. "We haven't set a date yet. He's leaving everything up to me."

"He should have some input," her mother said.

"He mentioned we could have the wedding in Denver, but all of his co-workers and family live here."

"You have a lot of people here, too. The teachers you worked with, the faculty, your neighbors, Beth … But I think … Dodge City is your home, now. You should have it there. We'll come there."

"Thanks, Mom. That means so much to hear that. I was racking my brain, trying to figure out how to please everyone. Talk about my OCD kicking in." A weak smile curled up on her lips.

"No need to please anyone but you and Sam. Your happiness is all that matters."

Wow, this new and improved Marjorie really hit her to the core of what it meant to be a supportive parent. Maybe she took heed of what she'd said during her meltdown when they'd met Sam. "Mom, you surprise me all the time how strong of a woman you really are. You are the nucleus to this family. You back off when you should, and go in when you need to. You treat us with kid gloves if the situation calls for that, and you also pull on the boxing gloves when we need that, too," Lucy said, feeling sorry she'd ever doubted her mother's strength.

"Lucy, dear," she said, not letting her finish. "That's what mothers and wives do. I'm strong when I need to be and nurturing all the time. You see, I know you know the difficult times your father and I went through. You were right there. But after you moved out and went to college, I was left alone to deal with a lot of stuff—some really heavy stuff that I don't want to share right now. But suffice it to say, your dad is a great guy, and I wouldn't have hung around as long as I did if I didn't know that. Every day I saw him give more of himself, grow as a human being, and it takes a strong woman to know that. Not a weak one—a strong one. I love him, for better or worse. Now grant you, if it had gotten any worse, I'd have skedaddled right out of here."

"Mom, thanks for sharing all of this with me today. I really needed to hear it. I've been pretty insecure in my life. But Sam … Sam brings out strength in me I didn't know I had. In the beginning, I was filled with so much emotion I couldn't get a grip on it. I think I might have driven him away if I hadn't straightened up my act when I did."

"He knew you were worth it. Just like I knew your dad was."

"I love you and Dad and I'm just glad we didn't end up like some statistic."

"He's a different man, but the same. Does that make sense?"

"Totally. And I'm happy for you two."

"Now, plan the prettiest wedding Dodge City has ever seen. Oh, and, Lucy?"

Lucy blinked. "Yes?"

"Send the bill to your father."

CHAPTER 21

With Lucy wedding dress shopping in Denver with her mother and Beth, Sam decided a trip to the fire station to pump some iron would be in order. However, when Charlie grunted and rolled over, exposing his tummy for a rub, Sam knew that also was code for take me for a walk. He grabbed the leash off the hook and the two bounced out the door for what should have been an uneventful walk.

"A quick run around the path and then that's it, Charlie," he said as they jogged.

But they didn't get too far when Charlie put on the brakes and began to breathe hard. Sam had been trained well enough to know when someone, be it a human or a dog, was in distress. He leaped over and began stroking him on the head. "Are you alright, big guy?"

Poor Charlie grunted and gasped, his tongue hanging out as he tried to breathe. Sam scooped him up and ran with him, trying to get to his truck quickly. He drove like a madman to the emergency vet.

Breathing heavily himself, Sam rushed in with Charlie in his arms, pleading for help. "Please, my dog … he's having trouble breathing."

The clerk rushed around and took Charlie out of Sam's arms, leaving him standing there bewildered. He took a seat in the waiting room, his own heart beating wildly as he went over the details in his mind of what just took place.

He leafed through a few magazines as he waited for word. Finally, a tall, thin woman wearing a white doctor coat approached him. Her voice soft and congenial, she asked him to follow her.

She motioned for him to take a seat opposite of her. She placed her elbows on the desk. A warm sympathetic smile crossed her lips as she began to speak. "Charlie has some fluid around his heart. We've given him some meds to make him comfortable."

"I see. What does this mean exactly?"

"Well, he has congestive heart failure."

Sam's jaw dropped.

"We can treat the symptoms, but he's not going to get

better. I would suggest he lose a little weight, too. I can recommend some great low-calorie food for him."

"So, he's not going to die?"

"Not yet. Now, if you would prefer to—"

Sam vehemently shook his head. "No! I don't want to put him down. Unless he's in pain …" He looked at the vet for answers.

She rolled her head a bit. "He was in pain, but we've managed to help with that with the medication. If you're prepared to administer meds to him on a daily basis and get him a bit more exercise, I think he'll be around for a bit longer."

Sam slumped in his chair. "Man, this is really a hard blow to deal with right now. I'm getting married soon and I'm a fireman, so I'm rarely home. My sister takes care of Charlie a lot for me."

"It's a lot to think about, and no one would think badly of you if you decide on the alternative, especially us here. We know not everyone has the time or the money to take care of sick animals. That's what we are here for, to help." Her eyes softened and made him feel a bit better about all of this.

"I don't think I'm ready to let him go."

She pushed her chair back and stood. "I think he's going to be okay if you follow my advice. Every animal, if he or she lives long enough, develops some sort of heart problems. We do, too." She walked around the desk and laid her hand on his shoulder.

Sam nodded. "I'll do whatever you say."

"Good enough. And if, for some reason, you don't see any improvement, bring him back in. We might have to adjust his meds a bit before we get it right, just like doctors do for humans." She walked him out of her office.

"Can I see him?"

The vet opened another door off the hallway. Sam followed closely behind. They entered a large room where a few technicians were busily looking at samples under microscopes and tending to animals in cages. Sam spotted Charlie right away. He was in a ground kennel wagging his tail.

"Oh, Charlie," Sam said, kneeling down.

The vet opened up the cage and let Charlie come out. He immediately licked Sam's face. Sam laughed. "He seems better already." He ran his hand along Charlie's back, and rubbed behind his ears. "You're not ready to toss in the towel, are you, old boy?" He roughed up his coat some more and then hugged him.

"I'd like to keep him overnight, if that's okay. Just to monitor him. You can pick him up tomorrow morning."

Sam brushed his hand along Charlie's head. "Sure."

Sam watched as the vet placed Charlie back inside the

roomy cage. "We'll go over his medication and diet tomorrow." Her smiling eyes lifted the heaviness from his shoulders and his heart.

He pulled out his hand to meet hers. "Thanks, Doc, for everything."

"You got him here quickly. That was key in saving his life." She walked him out to the main reception area.

He waved to her and the clerk behind the desk that so gallantly took Charlie from him, and then walked out into the autumn air. He noticed the yellow leaves as they drifted and swirled before finally dropping to the ground where all the leaves were beginning to pile. Once inside his car, he shed a few tears. Lucy's sensitive side was beginning to rub off on him.

He drove over to the station to see who was on because he didn't want to be alone. He didn't want to ruin Lucy's weekend with the girls either, so he felt it would be better to wait and tell her about Charlie later. The guys would understand. They loved dogs. Their love for their dogs was right up there with their love for their wives and kids. Well, almost.

To avoid going back to his lonely apartment, he joined them for dinner even though he wasn't on the clock. After dinner, he settled into one of the leather recliners in the station's living room and watched reruns of Game *of Thrones*. After a few episodes, he headed home.

He didn't like to be alone and he didn't like to drink alone, but tonight was a bit different. He poured some scotch in a small glass, about two-fingers' worth, and while sipping on the amber colored liquor he channel surfed. When Lucy called, he started off by asking her all about her shopping trip.

"I found the most perfect dress, Sam." Her excitement radiated through the phone.

"That's great, hon. I'm happy. So you're having a good time with your mom and Beth? No drama, right?" He chuckled.

"It's been a fairly drama-free zone," she acknowledged. "What about you? What have you been up to? Do you miss me?" The sensual tenor of her voice wafted through, causing him to miss her even more.

"I've been better." He couldn't keep this from her. Not something as important as Charlie—no way. "It's Charlie."

"What happened to Charlie?" she asked, her voice raising an octave.

"We went for a jog today and he about passed out. I rushed him to the emergency vet, the one over on

Calhoun … anyway, they ran some tests and determined it was his heart."

"Oh, Sam, I'm so sorry."

"I made the decision to start medication and also change his diet. The vet recommends he lose a little weight. I know this comes at an awful time with the wedding and all, but I asked Wanda to help, and she will. I hope you understand."

"Of course, Sam. I know Charlie is very important to you. I'll do whatever I can do to help. He's not in pain, right?"

"No, the vet assured me that she was able to drain the liquid, and hopefully with the medication he'll be around for a little bit longer. I got to see him; he was wagging his tail and everything."

"That's great. So you don't worry about a thing. I got this wedding thing all under control. You just worry about Charlie."

"Thanks, babe. I love you. I wish you were here with me. I'm feeling a bit blue without Charlie."

"I'll be home tomorrow afternoon. I love you, Sam Lyons. I always will."

Sam tossed his phone on the coffee table and picked up his drink. He thought about how his life had changed and for the better, and it all started when he met a pretty little thing from Denver. He drew in another sip.

He went from being happy and single, to happy and engaged, and now soon to be married. *I'm going to be married. Attached. Never single again.* As much as he wanted this it scared him, too. *That was totally natural, right?*

CHAPTER 22

They'd spent the better part of two days polishing up the trucks. Pete and the crew made sure the firehouse glowed from a thorough and deep cleaning, while Scotty recruited the wives to decorate and help with the food. It was all a family affair, anyway, so everyone was happy to pitch in for Sam and Lucy.

As a special wedding gift to the happy couple, they sent a cleaning crew up to the old fishing cabin and gave it a total makeover for the honeymooners. A proper honeymoon was in the works, when Sam and Lucy could get more time off, but in the meantime, neither of them could think of a better place to honeymoon than where he'd asked her to be his wife.

Exactly thirty days from when he'd proposed, Lucille Olivia Carmichael and Samuel Paul Lyons exchanged vows.

Standing under a white arbor, laced with an abundance of flora in burnt orange, yellow, and green, Lucy and Sam held hands as the preacher read from the Good Book. When he looked at them to continue, Sam went first.

He held her hands snug in his, feeling the warmth run through his veins. He swallowed down his nerves, focusing on her beautiful green eyes, and soon the words began to dribble out like a waterfall yearning for rain. "Lucy …" He paused.

She gently squeezed his hands to give him encouragement to continue, and it was just what he needed, because then the words began to flow like a stream after a huge rain shower.

"I want our marriage to be special. I always want us to be truthful with one another."

She nodded.

"I'll always support you in whatever you do, but most importantly, I'll be by your side during the sweet times and during the difficult times. And no matter what hill we have to climb, no matter what … I'll always love you."

A few tears glistened in her eyes as she heard his

sweet words. Then it was her turn. "Sam Lyons." She giggled. "I think I fell in love with you the moment I first laid eyes on you, if that's possible." She blushed. "I know we have some things to overcome, but I'm telling you, here and now and in front of all your crew, that I'll do my part to make it work. Should I behave like a spoiled new wife who doesn't understand what her hubby does for a living, I expect you to … just to love me through it all. See me for my good qualities and not just my imperfections." She lowered her gaze.

He reached out and lifted her chin and mouthed *I love you.*

Then the preacher pronounced them husband and wife. Sam pulled Lucy in for one heart-throbbing kiss that made a few of the firefighters play a prank by pretending to spray them with water from a hose. All the guests broke out laughing and chanted, "Put out the fire!"

It was a gorgeous November day. The air was crisp with a bright blue sky above and hardly a cloud in sight. The crowd stood in single file as they dished up food spread out on long tables donned with white linen and decorated with centerpieces of mums in orange and yellow. It was all easy and casual, just as they'd planned it. It was the best way everyone could attend, and yet still be on standby if they were called to duty.

As the late afternoon approached, so did the cooler

temperatures. The party was winding down, anyway, but a few stragglers were hanging around.

"This is the only wedding I've been to where there was no alcohol available." Pete ran his hand along his chin as he contemplated this statement.

"We'll have another party later, but right now, this was the best way so that we could have all of you as part of our special day." Sam patted his buddy on the shoulder.

"Hey, Sam," Scotty said, reaching out to shake his hand.

Sam beamed as he looked over at Lucy huddled around her mom and dad, laughing.

"She's a great catch, Sam." Scotty crossed his arms and rocked back on his heels. "Now, you're part of the married club. You know what that means, right?" He winked at Pete then turned his eyes back to Sam.

Sam laughed then realized they were serious. "No," he said slowly. "What does that mean?"

"It means no more taking extra shifts for us. You're one of us now. That means we take some of yours, too. We're all in it together."

"That's all fine and good, but we could use the extra money. We're just starting off. We'd like to buy a house and that takes money."

"Well, since you put it that way …" He looked over at Pete who was nodding. "You got yourself a deal."

"If you guys will excuse me, I want to go steal a kiss from my beautiful bride."

Pete crossed over to Scotty and the pair watched as one of the youngest on their crew, and now the newlywed of the bunch, quickly reached his bride, pulling her in for a hug and kiss.

"Get a look at that. Aren't they so cute?" Pete said, smiling.

"Yep, and so gullible, too." Scotty chuckled, making Pete study him hard. Scotty rolled his head toward Pete and arched his brows.

"You didn't!"

Scotty nodded. "And he bit it, hook, line, and sinker."

"You're not going to let him take all the extra shifts, are you?"

"Only until he figures out he's been duped." Scotty slung his arm around Pete and the two moseyed over to a small crowd of guests who were roaring in laughter and having a good time.

"Now, Charlie will probably bug you to take him for a walk. He'll go over to his leash and just sit staring at it,"

Lucy explained to her parents as they settled into their car.

"If you need anything, call Wanda. We won't have any cell coverage, or at best, it will be sporadic," Sam said, shutting the car door.

"We'll be fine. You two should be getting up there soon. It'll be dark and the roads—"

"Mother," Lucy said, cutting her off. "We'll be just fine. You and Daddy drive safely back to the apartment." She kissed her mother on the cheek then walked around to the driver's side where Sam and Paul were laughing.

All of a sudden, Lucy stopped dead in her tracks, gasping and covering her mouth.

"What's wrong?" Sam said with alarm in his voice.

"I just realized something as I watched you and Dad laughing and talking."

Paul craned his head out the window and studied his daughter, a look of surprise on his face. "Oh, and what was that?"

"Sam's middle name is Paul." A slow smile escaped her lips.

Sam wrapped his arm around her and pulled her in, kissing the top of her head. "And you just realized this, really?" He chuckled loudly and then tickled her sides, making her laugh even harder.

"Yes, I just put it all together. I don't know why it took me until now."

Paul started the engine, and then raising his hand up in a wave, took off, leaving Sam and Lucy wrapped in each other's arms, smiling.

"Ready to go, Mrs. Lyons?"

His dashing good looks, amplified by his tux, made her melt and she wasn't sure if she could even speak without crying tears of joy. "Yes, Mr. Lyons, I am."

As they were bid farewell by the few remaining guests, Lucy and Sam stepped up into the freshly waxed rescue truck, ready to be driven by none other than Scotty. With lights flashing and sirens blazing in true Dodge City Fire Department fashion, Sam and Lucy Lyons began the first day of their new life together as husband and wife, cuddled in the back seat, stealing kisses and soft touches as they were chauffeured to the old fishing cabin.

"Okay, you kids, get out." Scotty put the truck in park, leaving it to idle.

Sam helped Lucy out as she tried to hold up the corners of her dress, keeping it as clean as possible. He reached in the back and grabbed their overnight bag, slinging it over his shoulder.

"We'll deliver your truck here later. No need to poke your head out or anything. We know you'll be busy." Scotty chuckled, and not waiting for a reply, he drove away, leaving the newlyweds standing there.

"Busy—I don't know what he's referring to, do you?" He suddenly lifted her, cradling her in his arms and making her squeal as she kicked her legs out.

It amazed her how easily he picked her up. She leaned back into his strong embrace as he stepped toward the front porch. With one quick move, he opened the door and carried her through the threshold.

Her eyes lit up. "Wow! They really did a number on this place."

He put her down. "I told them they'd better have it so clean that we could eat off the floors if we wanted to." Sam ran his finger along the furniture and showed her that there was no dust.

A broad smile appeared on her lips. "Well, they did a fine job."

He held out his arms. "Come here, you beautiful thing."

She waltzed into his arms, wrapping her arms around his waist. "I love you, Sam."

He held her back and stared into her eyes, wondering

if she really knew how much he loved her, how complete she made him feel. It was hard for him to put it into words, but he'd die trying to show her each and every day just how important she was to him. "Baby, I'm not good with words. Most guys are probably not, but I love you so much and I'll do my best to show you every day."

She rested back into his clasped hands and studied his face. "I know, baby. We'll be just fine."

Holding her face in his hands, time came to a standstill as he looked deeply into her eyes. He slid his arm around her waist to hold her in place, lowered his head, and when he felt his heart pound heavily in his chest, pulled her closer, meeting her warm and ever so inviting lips. He gently pressed her mouth open, encouraging soft moans from her. His own deep throaty groan surprised him as they devoured each other with deep, hot, and sensual strokes. He picked her up into his arms once again, and stumbled toward the bedroom, all the while their lips still locked and engaged in hungry kisses.

She unpinned her hair and let it fall softly around her shoulders. She fluffed it out with her hands, his breath catching as he watched his beautiful bride ready herself for him. He helped her out of her wedding dress, and then when he couldn't contain his hunger for her any longer, he lifted her up to lower her onto the bed.

He brushed away the strand of hair that fell into her

eyes. Convinced that her gorgeous eyes were the key to unlock the deep unabashed passion they had for one another, he didn't want anything to block his view of them. His open mouth came down on her just as they breathed a heady *I love you*, and then they closed their eyes, giving in to the desire and heavy ache between them.

CHAPTER 23

She took his hand and eased into the canoe with one foot then the other, feeling the boat wobble a bit before she took her seat opposite him. He picked up the oars and began to paddle. She held onto the sides of the aluminum boat as she took in the sights. The boat rippled quietly through the waters as Sam dipped the oars into the water and pushed them around the lake.

"It's so peaceful out here," he said as he smiled broadly at her.

"I love it. This time of year is one of my favorites. Look at all the colors in the trees." She motioned with her chin, not ready to let go of the sides of the boat just yet.

"You're not scared, are you?"

"I've never been in a boat before," she confessed.

"Wow, okay. I didn't realize that. Are you too uncomfortable, because if you are—."

She shook her head a few times. "No, don't be silly. I'm having a great time."

They had paddled for about fifteen minutes or so when he suddenly dropped the oars inside the canoe and jumped out onto the sandy shore, grabbing a rope and pulling the small craft up.

A shrill sound escaped her lips. "What … where are we?"

"Thought we could explore." He held out his hand for her to take hold.

They walked the quiet forest lined lake, weaving in and out of well-beaten paths, most likely from people but also from the abundant deer in the area. Every now and then, they could hear a twig break or sounds of leaves as they rustled to the ground. She gathered a few yellow and red ones, and a pinecone or two. Fortunately for her, she had come prepared with a gallon-sized plastic bag to store all her finds.

"Now, this is fresh air." She drew in a loud sounding breath, and then let it out just as loudly.

He grabbed her hand and drew her body close.

"What?"

Her eyes twinkled like little stars and melted his heart every time they danced. "This is what." He planted a kiss right on her mouth, kissing her like he never wanted to let her go. He could feel her body relax against his, urging the kissing to continue.

"I love you, Sam." She breathed in between his hot little kisses.

"I will never get tired of hearing it, either." He squeezed her tighter.

"Come on, let's explore. We can do more of that later in the cabin." She grabbed his hand and pulled him along deeper into the woods.

"Hear that?" Sam stopped in his tracks.

"Woodpecker?" Lucy guessed.

Sam nodded.

They walked a bit farther and came to a clearing in the woods. Just then, a loud snap had them both looking toward the sound. There, in the clearing, stood a deer.

"What a beautiful creature," Lucy whispered, gazing toward the still animal.

They watched for a few seconds before the deer leaped through the brush and quickly disappeared.

"I think we better head back. It's getting late. I'm hungry and thirsty." Sam turned around and began the trek back to the canoe.

Once back at the cabin, they both rummaged around the kitchen and found items their friends had stocked for them. They made grilled cheese sandwiches and tomato soup, although, neither of them were really that hungry … at least not for food.

"It's been the best two days, hasn't it?" She gazed lovingly into his eyes as he held her close.

"It really has. Now it's back to work and our new life together."

She loved how he held her snug, just in the crook of his arm. Waking up with him beside her was a dream come true. "I do miss the children. I hope they didn't give the substitute teacher too hard of a time."

"They did."

She pulled out from his embrace and rested on an elbow while she played with his hair with her free hand. "What makes you thinks so?"

"All kids give the substitute teacher a hard time. That's what kids do. It's like a code or something among them."

"I never gave any of my substitute teachers a hard time. I admired the difficult job they had stepping in for our primary teacher."

Sam knitted his brows. "Seriously? You admired them?"

Lucy stopped twisting his hair with her finger and sat

straight up. "Yes, and I'll make sure our children learn respect for their elders and community leaders at an early age." She tipped her head as she pursed her lips.

"Our children?" He bolted straight up and clasped his hands over the sheet.

She rolled her head and nodded. "You do want children, don't you?"

He drew in a deep breath. "I do want them some day."

"Sam," she took one of his hands and held it. "You'll be a great dad. I'm not talking right away … down the road a bit."

"I'm just worried about my job and how kids will fit in. But most of the guys at the station have families."

"I hear a bit of hesitation in your voice. I guess I just assumed we'd have kids. I guess we should have discussed this before we got married." She climbed out of bed and moved to the window, staring out with her arms crossed.

He followed her, wrapping his big arms around her waist. Kissing her shoulder, he gazed out the window with her. "You know I love you, Lucy. I guess I never thought about kids. Maybe we should have talked about that. It's a very important detail. I guess I always worried about the dangerous career I'm in and if it would be fair to bring children into the fold. I'm not saying I don't want them; I'm just saying I want to get used to being married for a while." He rocked her in his arms.

A tear rolled down her face but she was too stubborn to wipe it. She didn't want him to know she was shedding tears, especially from their first fight after only being married for two days. She sniffed back any more that tried to make their presence known.

He turned her around while still holding her. "Lucy Lyons, look at me." He raised her chin, stopping her from avoiding his eyes any longer.

Heaving a deep sigh, she bit down on her bottom lip.

"I love you," he said, not letting her move her eyes from him.

"I love you, too," she mumbled under her breath.

"I can't hear you," he teased, leaning forward and kissing her neck.

"I love you," she shouted.

"Okay, that's better. Let's put this behind us. We'll have plenty of time to talk about children. Right now, we have our careers, each other, and let's not forget old Charlie." He placed his hands on her shoulders. "Let's get packed and ready to head back home." He began to move away from her but was held back because she'd grabbed his hand.

"Sam."

All of his attention was on her.

"I agree we have lots of time, but I have to tell you that if I don't—can't—have your baby someday, I don't know what I'll do. I need that. I need that from you." Her eyes misted with the last word.

Just then the old lightbulb came on in his head. He'd heard similar talk among the fire crew. The women desired children because being the wife of a fireman was sometimes lonely, but also because it was dangerous. And in that moment, Sam realized Lucy wanted a baby because it would help keep his memory alive if something bad were to ever happen to him. A slow smile moved across his mouth. "I get you baby, I do." He pulled her in for one last steamy kiss before they got ready to hit the road going home.

THE NEWLYWEDS HAD a bit of adjusting to do, like most new couples. Sharing space when you previously had it all to yourself could be a bit … well, like a kid reluctantly sharing his toys. You had to kind of roll into it.

"Sam, Charlie is drooling all over my sofa pillows," Lucy complained.

"He can't help it." Sam propped his feet on the coffee table.

Lucy lifted his feet off and set them back down on the floor. "The table is not for feet."

Sam cut his eyes to her. "Come on, seriously?" He grunted in frustration over all the new rules.

"You know I run a tight ship around here." Lucy raised her brows, waiting for further rebuttal from him.

"I know you do, dear, but seriously … no feet on the coffee table?"

She snuggled under his arm, lifting up slightly to kiss his chin. "I love you, Sam, but I have certain things that drive me crazy. Feet on the table, dirty clothes on the floor, wet towels wadded up in the corner—"

"And drooling dogs," Sam interjected.

"I can live with a little drool," she whispered when she looked over at Charlie who was curled up in a ball and snoring softly. "He can't help it, you're right. But you can make sure your clothes make it into the hamper." She patted him on his thigh.

"I'll learn to be more of a guest and less of a slob."

"Guest? This is your home, too. I just …" She shook her head.

He cupped her hand with his. "Just give me a little time. I've been a bachelor for a while and never shared a place with anyone except another messy guy." He winked.

"Take all the time in the world. I love you for better

or worse, sloppy or tidy. As long as you're here with me, I can live with anything."

"I'M LATE FOR WORK," Lucy said, leaning over for a quick kiss.

"Have a great day. Love you," he called out from under the covers.

He waited a few minutes after he heard the front door close. He lifted off the covers and crawled out of bed stretching before he dressed in some shorts and a comfy tee shirt. After a cup of coffee and a light breakfast, he took Charlie for a walk, emptied the dishwasher, making sure to put all the dishes away in the right cabinets, stripped the bed and put clean sheets on it, then dusted all the living room tables, wiped up any drool from Charlie, and ran the vacuum. He jumped in the shower and dressed in her favorite faded jeans and baby blue tee shirt that she'd told him time and time again did something to his eyes. For a final touch, he lit some vanilla candles, popped a frozen lasagna into the oven, opened a bag of pre-made salad, and sliced some French bread. He made sure a bottle of their favorite wine was ready for pouring, and then he sat back on the sofa and waited for the love of his life to come home.

He rolled his head toward the sound of the door opening.

Her nose wrinkled and then she smiled. "Something smells wonderful." She looked around the apartment.

He patted the sofa. "Come sit."

She tossed her purse on a peg on the hall tree and sat next to him. "You've been busy." She stole a kiss.

He nodded. "I vacuumed, dusted, changed the sheets, and have dinner ready." His boyish grin matched his juvenile tone.

"I'm impressed. Sam … this isn't about the other night is it? Because I—"

He sealed her mouth with a deepening kiss, not allowing her to finish. "No, you were right. I wasn't playing house nicely. This is me, showing you that I love you and I care. I'll never be quite as fastidious as you when it comes to housework, clothes, or even grooming, but I'm trying."

She took his hand in hers. "Sam, I love you so much. Just you trying, means so much to me. Thank you. I'm going to work on being less picture-perfect, because I'm not really perfect, I just think I am. I want to be a regular person." She kicked off her shoes and propped her feet on the coffee table.

Sam's eyes widened. "Wow. That's a big move right there." He nodded toward her stocking feet.

He rose from the couch, picking her feet up and pulling her legs to the cushion, gently setting them down. She watched him intently through narrowing eyes as he made his move. Then he rolled up on top of her, being careful not to put all of his weight on her. He slowly shook his head in utter disbelief over how lucky he was to have her. Tucking a lock of hair behind her ear, he moved toward her mouth, slowly swiping his lips across hers and making her groan softly. She closed her eyes and took him in, deeply enjoying how he felt. Their bodies fit like a well-worn glove. After a few moments of very satisfying kisses and touches, he rolled off of her, leaving her breathless and warm all over.

"Come on, let's have dinner." He held out his hand to her, a deep longing still visible in his baby blue eyes—the ones that his shirt matched so well.

She took his hand as he helped her up, and slipped her arm around his waist as they walked into the kitchen.

"I was hoping we'd really step out of the box and have dessert before dinner." She tilted her chin up and gave him a sexy look.

*L*iving in Dodge City transformed Lucy's life in more ways than she'd ever imagined. She recalled the day the tourism department had notified her via letter that she'd been the lucky recipient of the prize package due to the essay she'd submitted on why she wanted to visit Dodge City. She'd always been a great writer with a vivid imagination, so when she'd put pen to paper and romanticized about everything from moonlight barn dances to watching the fast-paced and thrilling rodeo, she must have gotten their attention. And boy, was she ever glad she did.

Sam worked many long hours with little time off. Fire season seemed to get worse with each summer. Battling blazes from lightening, or other acts of Mother Nature couldn't be prevented, but when some bozo was to blame, that changed everything. It was one thing to destroy someone's property, but to risk lives, too, that was unconscionable in her eyes and in the eyes of the other wives, as well.

She found herself traveling to Denver by herself more often than she wished. But he'd insist she go visit her folks while he pulled a three-day shift, and if it happened to fall on a weekend, she did. Sometimes the four walls came crashing in on her, so *getting out of Dodge* seemed to be the answer.

It was on one of her trips to Denver that she had to pull over to the side of the road to vomit. It must have been the breakfast sandwich she ordered from the fast-food place before she took off for the day. Wiping her mouth with the stack of napkins they'd wastefully supplied her with, she ventured back on the road and soon arrived at her parents' house.

"Your coloring is off, Lucy," her mother remarked. "Are you feeling alright?" She placed her hand on her forehead.

"I felt fine until I ate that darn breakfast sandwich." She opened the fridge and peered inside, grabbing the orange juice.

"Your dad is off playing golf. He made some new friends." Her mother's voice smacked of happiness, making Lucy shake her head.

"How'd he meet these friends?" She brought the ice-cold juice to her lips and tasted it.

"Through church. I'm just so happy he's made the leap. He thinks he has to do everything with me. I really need the space." She pulled out a chair at the kitchen table, and nodding to Lucy, sat down. "How's Sam?" Her eyes lit up.

Lucy picked up her glass of orange juice and joined her mother at the table. "He's good—working a lot. I see him while he's sleeping next to me." She shrugged.

Marjorie patted her hand. "He's doing what he loves."

"I know. And I'm thankful he has such a great job. I'll eventually get used to it. I'm still finding my way, too."

"Friends? Are you making many?"

"Yes. The wives of the other firemen have been so good to me. We meet about once a month for lunch. Then there is Arletta. We see each other occasionally, as well." She played with the rim of her glass. "It's all fine and good, but I miss Sam."

"Lucy … are you okay?"

Lucy pushed back her chair and ran for the bathroom, holding her hand over her mouth. Her mother sat in the chair with her arms crossed as she heard her daughter vomiting in the bathroom. A warm smile spread across her mouth.

"I don't know what's wrong with me." Lucy came out, drying her hands on a towel.

"I know what's wrong with you."

HOLDING SAM'S HAND, they stood in front of the plate glass window, staring in.

"I didn't think they'd ever leave," Sam chuckled.

"They're just so happy for us," Lucy said, her eyes glued to the little acrylic bassinet that held a baby swathed in a blanket.

He squeezed her hand as he looked down at his pride and joy. "Are you sure about the name?" He turned his head and studied her profile. She didn't take her eyes off of the baby, but she nodded once.

"Because we don't have to name him that. I'm perfectly happy going with Scotty or Pete."

She cut her eyes to him, and when she realized he was teasing her, they broke out in laughter. "I'm very serious."

"CONGRATULATIONS, SAM," the crew said, taking turns handing him bubble gum cigars.

Holding up the one lone pink cigar, Sam asked, "Hey, what's with this one?"

"That's for the next one. We're thinking ahead."

The entire fire station fell out with boisterous laughter.

Sam shook his head. "Let me get used to the first one." But he had to admit, he loved the idea of having a son, especially one named after him.

WHILE THE WOMEN took turns holding Sam Jr., Lucy sat back and enjoyed watching all of them fondly adore him. *Their new son.* She was getting used to saying it and thinking it. Now they were a family of three.

Her mother seemed to be burning up the roads between Denver and Dodge City. She couldn't get enough of her new grandson. Her dad came, too, but when he saw all the women, he would quietly leave the apartment with Charlie.

Lucy, happy for the distraction from the visitors, knew all too well that she'd be left alone soon enough with her thoughts, fears, and loneliness, knowing her husband would be gone for a few days. When a fire broke out, she'd keep Sam Jr. close, hoping for the best, and when Sam walked through those doors she would finally breathe and they could be a family again, until it was time for him to leave again.

WHEN SAM JR. turned three years old, Lucy got a touch of the flu, or so she thought. Her eyes widened and then she gasped, a broad smile soon warming her face. She stepped inside the bedroom and watched as Sam slept. He'd just gotten off a long shift. She sashayed over to the bed and dropped down on the mattress, bouncing it a few times.

Sam stirred then rubbed his eyes, and slowly opened them. "Hey, babe." His voice laced with sleepiness, but grinning as his eyes closed.

She bounced again.

He quickly opened his eyes. "What's up?" The sheepish grin on her face told him something was definitely up.

"I'm pregnant."

"Oh, that's good, honey." He closed his eyes again.

She cocked her head as she raised her brows. She counted silently. On the count of four he opened his eyes and blinked.

"Did you say—?"

She leaned over and kissed him, stopping his flow of words.

He pulled her over on top of him. "We're going to have another baby?"

She nodded. "I think so. I'm late, and I just hurled my breakfast. The last time I did that, I was pregnant with Sam Jr."

"I love you, Lucy. My life is so complete now."

She tilted her head and with a look of concern said, "How so?"

"A boy and a girl—our family will be complete."

"I don't know if it's a girl, Sam. It could very well be another boy. But as long as they are healthy, I don't care what it is."

"True. I guess I was hoping for a little Lucy." His eyes twinkled as he spoke her name.

"Now, now. Don't think for a second we're going to name her after me. One Lucille Olivia Lyons is enough." She tossed her head back and laughed.

"Are you kidding me? The world needs more Lucille Olivia Lyonses."

Her eyes began to mist. "Sam, you always know the right thing to say." She leaned forward and dropped a quiet kiss on his mouth. When she tried to move back, he held her in place, kissing her back.

"This calls for family togetherness." He gently moved

her off of him, tossed off the sheet, and stood, stretching and yawing.

Lucy, bewildered with his actions, studied his face. "Family togetherness?"

"Wake up Sam Jr. and pack a lunch. We're going out for the day. How about the zoo?"

"Sam, you haven't had enough sleep. What about your rest?"

"Rest is overrated. I want to be with my little family."

Lucy walked over to the doorway and held onto the frame, turning her body slightly. Her eyes followed him as he made his way toward the shower, to wash the cobwebs out of his brain, most likely, and to breathe some life into him so he could function at the zoo, no less. Her heart swelled with so much love for the two guys in her life, and soon, for the new edition to the Lyons' household.

"Hey, Sam," she called out, just as he stepped into the adjoining bathroom.

He turned his head toward her.

"What if I'm not pregnant? What if it's a false alarm?"

The smoldering sexy look in his eyes told her everything she needed to know. She nodded, and then headed for the kitchen to pack their picnic lunch.

A Note from the Author

If you're ready to go on to the next book in the series, California Crush, follow the link. Happy reading!

Debbie

www.ingramcontent.com/pod-product-compliance
Lightning Source LLC
Chambersburg PA
CBHW070523100726
47907CB00004B/961